Ludwig's Room

Ludwig's Room

ALOIS HOTSCHNIG

Translated by Tess Lewis

LONDON NEW YORK CALCUTTA

This book has been selected to receive financial assistance from English
PEN's 'PEN Translates!' programme, supported by Arts Council England. English PEN exists to promote literature and our understanding of
it, to uphold writers' freedoms around the world, to campaign against the
persecution and imprisonment of writers for stating their views, and to
promote the friendly co-operation of writers and the free exchange of
ideas. www.englishpen.org

This publication was supported by a grant from the Goethe-Institut,
India

Seagull Books, 2014

First published in German as *Ludwigs Zimmer* by Alois Hotschnig © 2000,
Verlag Kiepenheuer & Witsch GmbH & Co. KG, Cologne

English Translation © Tess Lewis, 2014

ISBN 978 0 85742 2 040

British Library Cataloguing-in-Publication Data

A catalogue record for this book is available from the British Library

Typeset by Seagull Books, Calcutta, India

Printed and bound by Hyam Enterprises, Calcutta, India

I should never have accepted the inheritance, that's when it all began. This house had made others unhappy before me. I should never have moved in, should have simply avoided Landskron and Villach, even Carinthia altogether, from the very beginning. And yet, I did seek out this house. I entered it and took over and at the same time, cut myself off from everything that had mattered to me until then. I adopted Landskron and left Vera. I fled everything I possibly could and chose this place to hide in, as refuge, and ensconced myself here. Hiding, for me, was always a pleasure and I indulge in that passion here. I had to wait a long time, I waited for years as my predecessors in this house died out and all that time, from a safe distance, I tried to adapt myself to this house and this place and I did and the time finally came. With Anna's death, the door finally stood open. I turned the latch and moved in. Over the years, I'd observed Landskron and prepared myself for it, but I had completely misjudged things and wasn't at all prepared for what I would find. The house, a cabin actually, was run-down, neglected, falling apart. When I opened the door, the smell enveloped me and sucked me right in. The previous owners had all died but hadn't yet left. They were still here. I could feel them. They'd waited for me for years and they welcomed me now with this odour that drew me from one room to the next. It's my childhood, I thought. The mildew, the stench will wash over me and cling to me and finally even seep out through me and so become my odour, as it had been before.

I should never have come here, not even back then as a child, but I couldn't help it. My uncle, my great-uncle actually, would call, we must come, so we came. He and Anna held court here. They summoned me and my parents and they summoned the others as well, all the relatives and their children, once a year, twice. For the parents it was an obligation, an honour, and for the children a chore. *When we head over to Landskron you must clean yourselves up, you have to be neat and well groomed.* So we arrived for Uncle's pictures spruced up and well groomed. Uncle invited us all and held court, summoning all his relatives to the house, his *younger relations.* What none of us knew then was that he'd already begun choosing an heir and was bringing the *candidates* to his house, to consider them there. You can't begin the process too early, he told me later. No one knew the real reason for those invitations at the time. The procedure was always the same—at some point, Uncle took me by the arm and led me out of the house and round it several times. I want to see how you're developing, how you're all developing, he'd say. Everything comes out in my photographs, nothing escapes them, he'd say and he'd lead me along the outside wall, looking for the spot best suited to me at that particular age. He would stop, place me against the wall and leave me standing there endlessly, facing him. Then he would put his finger in his mouth, always the same, wet it and smooth a strand of hair away from my forehead, always the same, whether there was a loose strand or not. He would tap me on the forehead with his finger, press my head against the wall and go back a few steps to look at me from a distance. He would get ready to shoot but would not take the picture. Then he would after all, once he'd finally seen everything, was finally sure he'd missed nothing, had finally calibrated my development; only after it had all become clear to him did he shoot.

I have to warn you about the Villachers, the woman from Villach said and introduced herself as one of my neighbours. On the day before Anna's funeral, she suddenly appeared in the room. The people who had taken care of Anna had refused to give me the house keys, too much was unclear and had to be straightened out first, so I had the locks changed. That's how I got in. I'd not been in the house even an hour and was already ferreted out in my hiding place.

Maybe you don't know that this house belongs to many people, at least many seem to believe that it does. But you'll see, she said, you have to protect yourself from people here. You don't know the Villachers. You're only the heir, you understand, no one has much to say about you here, not much that's good, anyway. People round here are concerned, so much is undecided, what's to become of the house and the wood and the land, of it all. I hope you're not thinking of moving in here, to Landskron, she said, whatever you do, don't do that. You're not to be blamed for the previous owners' misfortune but you'll be settling into your own if you move in here. Stay away from this place, just as you've stayed away for years at a time until now. It's what they expect of you. People here appreciate absence, so keep away as you've done until now. We're used to life without you and life will go on without you, as it has until now, at least that's how people figure it here, but you'll see soon enough. You don't know the Villachers, she said and led me out of the house and down to the dock. If you really do plan on staying and don't want the process to do you in, don't let anyone from Villach set foot on your land. You must know that the Villachers love their lake and will turn on anyone who restricts their access to it. They won't let you chase them off. Every now and again, some outsiders showed up and tried to worm their way in, she said, by making themselves indispensable, first to your uncle and then to your aunt. Things didn't end well for any of them. And it will be exactly the same with you, the real heir. Again and again, outsiders came and tried to worm their way in with your aunt and they'll try to worm their way in with you too, you'll see. It didn't do any good, believe me, they all failed. The last one, you see, on this spot right where we're standing, a dentist from Treffen, he knelt down on the dock, right here, because he'd got his hopes up, because he didn't know you'd legally incapacitated your aunt long before, as people say round here. I saw it myself, from my window, how he rolled Mrs Reger in her wheelchair down the hill to the lake and knelt down before her. He spread his arms wide and he said—I could hear it all the way up at my house. I'm just letting you know that when something is said down by the lake I can hear every word up there, so be careful. I didn't miss a single word— this is paradise, he said. Mrs Reger just smiled. They all say that here, she told him. But it *is* paradise, the dentist shouted and raised his arms again to the sky. With those words he dropped dead, right where you're standing. A beautiful day, I heard Mrs Reger say.

We've seen that kind of death often round here, the woman said and disappeared.

When I woke, it was day but not raining as it had been in my dream. I got up and found my bearings, which took me a while. It looked like the rain would set in again and I decided to track down the noise I'd been hearing. I stepped out in front of the house, where I could hear it more clearly. It seemed to be coming from one of the huts, from one of the sheds in front of which Uncle had always photographed the female candidates. The locks that I'd replaced the day before had been cut and the door to the shed stood open. A man was busy in some kind of workshop with what seemed to be metal sheeting. His confidence as he moved around the shed impressed me, so I watched him for a while. Since he gave no sign of letting me interrupt him, I ventured into the shed and sat on a stool next to him and continued to watch.

I must tell you, it's not very neighbourly of you, Mr Homeowner, he finally said without looking me in the eye or turning even slightly in my direction. To lock me out of my own workshop like that, you won't get close to anyone that way, he said. And, just so it's clear from the beginning, no one will lock me out of here again.

But who are you? I said, I don't even know you.

Well, that's just it, said the man. People round here have the advantage. You know nothing about us. You don't know your neighbours. You should do something about it or things will get tight for you here, that I guarantee. You should go out and meet people.

Death creeps round the house, my new neighbour's mother said when I stopped by to introduce myself. First the neighbour to our left, then Mrs Reger, your aunt, it doesn't bear thinking about. It's not a good time for any of us here on the lake. Mrs Reger didn't have an easy time of it. What a life! If it were me, thank you very much, I'd rather pack it all in and be done. But would that make anything better? I mean, one can hope, one should never lose hope, not ever, but still, if you look round, I tell you, it's better not to know anything or you really will want to leave. My son did a lot for Mrs Reger, at least as much as he could, I mean, towards the end you couldn't get near her. But people did try, you know. A gesture, whenever an opportunity arose. But not towards the end, as I said. They shut him out. Nothing but slander, as if he had ever expected anything in return. But people round here—I don't know what contacts you've got, but he was simply shut out from one day to the next, I mean, I'm not making any claims but up to that point he did everything for your aunt. And she often came here, to visit us, I'll have you know. We got along famously, it wasn't always the way it's been the past few years. They cut us off from her completely. My husband and Mr Reger were in the war together. When you're prisoners of war together, you understand, that forges a bond, they got along well. Mrs Reger created her own prison here, but what can you say, you have to be happy and content. Who knows what the future will bring.

Those people who surrounded your aunt, they've got to go. That's what we always said. But now that it concerns us again, I mean, my son surely won't bother you and you'll need someone who's familiar with everything and who can lend you a hand with this enormous property.

Or is he going to be shut out again? My son practically grew up at Mr Reger's house. Between you and me, that nice Mr Reger couldn't hit a nail on the head. He wasn't very handy, you know. You've got to defend yourself against these people and you're certainly not wasting time. If you turn on my son, then you're after the wrong man. Besides, who'd have thought we'd ever have to deal with you, so soon, too. Your aunt barely a week in the ground and you've already moved into the house. With all due respect, that doesn't seem very tactful. You'll remember us yet, you'll come back to the fold. That much is certain.

As she spoke her eyes were constantly drawn to the lake, where a group of men could be seen near the bank, in the reeds, trying to drag a lifeless body from the water with hooks.

By the end of January, the lake freezes, she said. Now they've found another one. Every year one of them washes up here, at least one, and always right here, always on our side of the lake. The shady side, it's always been called, but that's not it, it's the current. They jump into the lake in Bodensdorf or in Sattendorf or Steindorf, don't forget Annenheim. But they're always found here and have to be fished out on our side, that's what's deceptive, she said. It's the current. Dead ducks, birds, everything ends up here. The current brings it all to us, it all washes up here. It's got nothing to do with shade. In the autumn, they all jump in on the sunny side of the lake, the locals, I'm not talking about tourists, she said. In the winter, they get pushed over here under the ice. They're just looking for a homeland, Mrs Reger always said. But we're no homeland here, not for just anyone who couldn't find peace somewhere else, if you know what I mean. You should pack up your things. They search for peace at the lake but they never find it, not here with us, not in that way. Look over there, how they're fished out with poles and with hooks. Is that the kind of peace anyone would want? Thanks all the same. It's just the current, in the spring they surface here on our side. I don't even like looking at the other shore any more—it all ends up here.

You're only truly *at home* where you've got someone in the graveyard, Anna always said.

My *homeland* in Villach is Anna, my *homeland* in Villach is Georg. I have two dead here, Section IV, Row 9, Number 12. For me this is no homeland. Someone who's deceased is no home, only someone you've missed. Anna moved in with Georg. I moved into her house but didn't find any peace.

When the time comes, you'll take care of the grave, she said, the house and the grave, it's all one. That much was true—in the last years this house became her death chamber.

I promised her everything. For after her death. She wanted nothing for herself when she was alive.

Will you be able to keep your promise? I wonder if you'll manage to maintain the house, she always said.

And she was right, I had a lot of practice at being inept. She said I was incompetent, a fly-by-night. No one could rely on me. No one ever did.

Section IV, Row 9, Number 12, a freshly dug grave, good soil, the cross and the flowers, all just as she wanted. Her grave was laid out and planted with flowers.

We had bought the lantern together. In this light, I'll be shining for you, from this spot here, when it has come to that, she said and laughed. That was a long time ago.

Once, I bent over the grave and opened the lantern to change the old light bulb. I was lost in thought, not paying attention to my hands, which suddenly began burning. The lantern was crawling with ants. They'd built their nests there. I cleared them out but the lantern still wasn't empty. The ants just kept coming, crawling over my hands and into my clothing. I took out one of the glass panes. Piles of eggs were layered in the grooves of the fixture. I scraped them out and crushed them underfoot. Panicked, the creatures tried to save their brood and swarmed all over my skin, into my hair, running over my eyes and into my ears. The entire grave mound was a seething, swarming anthill. I put a candle in the lantern and lit it to kill off the brood. I set it down in the middle of the swarm and left, rubbing and scratching my skin.

In my family there's a long history of suicide. But for each one that passed, another arrived, at least one. We'll never die out. The little that binds us—ineptitude, malice, unreliability—is, in fact, our strength.

Except Georg, not one of us has ever amounted to much. The only thing anyone in my family has ever managed to do is to own his own grave or, at best, the family plot. They all end up with us. We are raised, then we're buried and the graves get new owners. And I, Section IV, Row 9, Number 12, *my* domain, my Anna, my Georg, so I, too, now own a grave, until my time comes to use it.

Insofar as you choose a place to live, you choose a place for your grave, Anna always told me. You should know what you're getting yourself into. Once here, no one ever returns.

With the ants, it's best to just let them be, the owner of the grave next to mine told me. You have to make peace with the ants or they'll make your life hell. These creatures are a singular breed, just like the Villachers. I'm not from here. My husband, you know. They never warmed to me, these people. A different race. People always greet each other in graveyards, it's the same all over the world, in graveyards you acknowledge each other. But not here, not in Villach. Just look at those women over there, they go up to the graves with their watering cans full and return with them empty. They pass so many benches on the way. In any other graveyard you'd strike up a conversation. In Villach, they just sit on their benches, contemplating their losses, each on her own.

  You aren't from here either, she said, patting my hand as she spoke. You don't say anything either but you go after the ants. That gives you away. People here aren't satisfied with each other, they're not enough for themselves, so they always bring in a few outsiders. They lure the outsiders here however they can. It's the same elsewhere, too, I should know, but here, they bring you to this place and leave you to rot at their graves, just look at me. And you, how did they lure you here?

A legacy.

So you've inherited then, have you? Me, I got married. And do you have to live with these people?

No, not exactly, I said.

All the same. I had to live with my husband. My entire life, let me tell you. In what part of town did they trap you with the will?

Landskron.

Landskron has no graveyard. Villachers don't want to be buried in Villach. They'd all prefer the cemeteries in the neighbouring towns but they all end up here.

If I want to see you again, I asked the woman, where can I find you?

Section IV, Row 9, Bench 2, she said, but you're still much too young for the graveyard and I don't want to bring you here.

In Landskron, I've chosen my place and I won't ever go back. There was always a room in this house waiting for me. I went into the house and climbed the stairs to the hallway that only now, for the first time in so many years, seemed as long and as high as when I was a child. I went down the hall, past the spare bedrooms to the room that had drawn me more than any other from the moment I first set foot in this house. The door was locked.

In Landskron, you have to make your own way, Anna always said. Doors in Landskron won't open for you on their own. I forced the door open and entered the room. I felt my way to the window and opened the shutters. There was damp everywhere, like sweat. The light lay upon it as if on moss.

A table, a chair, a wardrobe and a bed. Everything in the room was draped in sheets, the wardrobe and desk were locked up and empty, cleaned out even while some-one was living here, I thought. From the desk I could see Georg's view of the dock, the reeds, the lake and the opposite shore, the houses and inhabitants there.

I was never allowed in this room. We were all for-bidden from entering. It was the only room in the house that was always kept locked.

What was my uncle up to in here when he unlocked the door and locked it again behind him, then paced for a while, every night, after which all was quiet for a long time in the room? It was always the same. They always put me in the room next to his, so with time it became *my* room.

I knocked once. May I come in? I asked Georg. Not as long as I live, I heard him say through the door, maybe one day, but now it's too soon.

We were not allowed in the room nor could we ask any questions, so rumours supplanted the truth. They said Uncle Paul killed himself in the room, *hanged himself*, they'd agreed at some point, long before my time.

And yet, Anna once referred to it as *Ludwig's room*. Who's Ludwig? I asked. Why does Uncle Georg always keep the door locked?

People are strange, you know, she said. Perhaps I'll tell you someday. The room has its history, and believe me, you'll hear more than enough about it yet, my goodness, soon enough. Promise me you won't believe everything they tell you about it and, above all, don't believe what they won't tell.

Who's Ludwig? I asked Georg. What do you do in his room every night?

Georg loved rowing on the lake in the evening, rowing over to the other shore and then following it past the reeds, all the way down to Steindorf and back across the lake to Ossiach. He liked to take me along and I always had the feeling on these trips that there was something he wanted to tell me. I spoilt the trips with my questions, I know that now. What do you do in that room every night? I asked. Who's Ludwig? No answer. After that question, he usually turned back and for the rest of the boat ride did not say a word.

On the way home as we got close to shore, I saw that he'd left his window open during our trips.

The landing ritual was always the same. Georg got out of the boat and went ahead up to the house. It was my job to take care of the boat. From the boathouse I saw him close the shutters on the bay window. From then on the house remained dark. I tied up the boat and went into the house, up the stairs to the hallway and into my room. I listened as hard as I could at the door or through the wall. There were footsteps for a while, then silence, broken by a rustling of paper, the scrape of a drawer and the groans of the chair.

I listened in the hallway until there were no more footsteps, no creaking of the floor. He seemed to be waiting. What on earth is he doing, I wondered. Hours later he came out and locked up. The sound often woke me.

Years later, I'd given up asking and once, when we were coming back across the lake in silence, Georg saw me look up at the window from the boat.

He turned the boat round towards Ossiach and rowed out again, out so far that I could see the monastery at the end of the lake.

The thing about Paul isn't true, he said, just as everything else they say about the room isn't true. You've stopped asking. When I go into my cell every night, when I close the door behind me and lock myself in there for hours, I'm trying to get away from something I just can't escape, at least not in this way, not by staring at it as if I were staring into an abyss. I will never be freed this way, despite all these years, it's clear to me each time I leave the room, but I always come back the next day.

We tied up at the dock in Ossiach and climbed the slope to the abbey. In the graveyard he led me to a tombstone enclosed by a fence near the church's outer wall.

A murderer lived in the abbey, he said. They buried him here. They say he showed up one day here at the monastery and from then on he lived as a monk in the cloister. For years up to his death, he didn't speak a single word, trying to atone for his guilt. That's what they say. Only on his deathbed did he confess to the abbot.

They'll bring you to my deathbed when the time comes, that is, if you're willing. Do you understand me, Kurt? he asked.

I did not understand but said I was willing.

Down to the lake, out on the dock and back and forth on the dock and again up to the house and round it, into the cabin, the sheds, the wood, during the day and at night, all week long, I went as if driven, into the house and back and forth inside the house. I made myself at home and the house took me in, one room, then the next, each day a different room, the same smell. I still didn't belong but the house no longer resisted me. Retreat, I thought, isolation, no more neighbours, no one from my former life. I'm finally alone with myself, that was bad enough but that's what I wanted.

I woke to a pounding on the door. It wasn't yet day and I saw a boy running through the garden to the gate, where a car was waiting for him. He got in and it drove away.

After a while, pounding woke me again. An old woman stood at the door, trying to get into the house. Her key didn't fit the lock, how could it? She kept beating on the door with her umbrella.

What do you want here at this hour? I called down from the window. Who are you?

Her eyes finally spotted me. What do you think I want? I live here, young man, if you would possibly be so kind as to make yourself helpful. This lock never worked anyway.

I gave up and closed the curtains. But the woman did not. When I was ready to leave the house hours later, she was still at the door. The woman was surely confused and had been abandoned on my doorstep like a pet.

You must know I once lived here, long before your time, there in the front, facing the lake, in the room with the bay window. That was a long time ago but, still, let's go up, she said and came in.

Without looking round or showing any interest in the rest of the house, she went straight upstairs. She took my arm, as if it were the most natural thing in the world, and led me to the room.

I would have come sooner, much sooner, she said. I'd have preferred never to have left the house at all but they wouldn't allow that. I don't have much time, things are gradually becoming hazy for me, you know.

You won't set foot in that house as long as Georg is alive, Robert always said to me, my son, you know. Then Georg died. As long as Mrs Reger lives in that house, you won't take a breath there, he said. And so I waited. And Anna lived a long time.

Robert says to me, this heir is just a spawn of your people. Robert doesn't approve of me being here now but he brought me all the same. Maybe this one's different, I told him, and, after all, he isn't guilty, not from the beginning.

This much was new and I was very interested in whatever it was I wasn't guilty of. For once, at least, I wasn't guilty of something from the outset.

I unlocked the door to the room. The woman was finally quiet. I stayed behind and watched her as she entered. The room was familiar to her and she made herself at home. She went to the window and gazed at the lake for a long time.

It looks different now, she said without turning round, but that changes nothing. You can't clear away what happened the way you clean up a room. And yet, that's what they've done. Cleared everything away, the way they disposed of people back then.

Everything but the desk. This desk used to be mine.

I followed her into the room and she didn't object.

I see you don't know anything, she said. I'll come back. If I may. Ludwig and I, you see. Please go now, leave me alone for a bit, yes, I've waited so long for this moment.

I didn't understand, so she led me out of the room, closed the door behind her and didn't come out again.

I waited all day but she didn't come out. In the evening, I left. When I came back the next morning, the room was empty.

On the calendar in the kitchen, time had stopped on 28th March. The following day time stopped completely for Anna. *Forest maintenance by Mr Kunz*, she had written on the calendar.

There was nothing they wouldn't do for your aunt. Now, right before my eyes, I had proof of what they'd done to her. The forest was in as bad a state as the house, as all of Landskron, for that matter, a wilderness whose squalor suited me perfectly. It was *my* squalor, since I'd never really taken care of Anna. From a distance, I sent whatever money was needed for her care and paid off my obligation. I tried to buy myself free but in truth I only made it possible for Anna to end up in the situation she did.

I continued exploring the house and the area round it. In the house time stood still, mothballed, covered with moss, in the wood time was overgrown with scrub. These were now my thickets and brambles and what had not grown there on its own had been dumped by my neighbours over the years. I had my hands more than full and was worried I'd never be done with it, not on my own, that was clear.

The woman came more often, in the evening or early morning. I left the door unlocked so she could come and go as she wanted. She did come and go into the room without a word. She made herself at home and no longer locked the door behind her.

So I wouldn't disturb her, I moved into the next room. Her search was more important than mine, after all. I didn't bother her and she didn't wake me when she came.

She wasn't really revived here, at least she didn't seem to be, yet it was good to see, as she walked through the garden, her step become lighter, more relaxed every time, and she no longer watched anxiously for the car coming to pick her up. After weeks, her first smile, from the car, and a shy wave through the rear window, so the driver wouldn't see.

The lake was Georg's deathbed. He went out in his boat one night and never came back. They found him the next morning in his boat, which had drifted on the waves and was bumping against the piles of the dock. They were carrying him out of the house when I arrived.

A beautiful death, Anna said, it's what he always wanted, to be able to stay out on the lake and not have to return to the room. I worried each time he went out, every night, that this time he wouldn't come back. This boat, she said, give it away. I've always been afraid of it. I knew one day it would bring him back dead.

What was he trying to escape—no point in asking Anna if Georg himself wouldn't say. Who am I to talk about it, you simply missed each other, she said.

At some point I became estranged from myself, detached somehow, years before, and since then I've been running alongside myself as if we'd had a falling out. Since then, I live with myself as with someone else, another person. In the morning, I want to get up but he stays in bed and so we both stay in bed, I next to him, inside him, because I am the weight that keeps his body from getting up. Often I think that he's the one who has given up, not I, but perhaps it's the other way round. In any case, we'll perish together and therefore alone.

You'll come back to the fold, that's certain. Even worse, I'd be here on my own and would have to get along with myself. And that's what I wanted—to be completely inaccessible, finally, and not able to reach anyone else either, no possible way out. That's what always drew me here, to this place. I wanted to break with my past and not have anyone here between me and myself as there always had been before. But this was a mistake, I soon realized, because I couldn't stand it.

I knew that in coming here, I'd have to destroy everything, otherwise I'd never really belong. So I began with the area right round the house.

I cleared out all kinds of wood and that revived me. The pine trees I'd hugged as a child, I now sawed down— the father tree, the aunt tree, the uncle tree. Each of us had our own tree planted here, that's what Georg wanted. At every visit we posed for pictures and we planted. The children were photographed, the adults planted themselves and with time, grew into a forest that was nothing but darkness, not a clearing in sight; not an inch had been spared Georg's rage for planting. Georg himself had always loved shadows. He only went over to the sunny side of the lake at night in his boat.

The garden had become our family tree and that's what I was chopping down now, my tree, too, which I'd planted myself once Georg had decided I was no longer a child. There didn't seem to be a tree for Ludwig anywhere in the wood.

I hewed open spaces from the overgrowth, clearings that expanded and let in the light. They were bare and drenched in light. As a child, I kept getting lost in this forest of relatives and Georg always forced me back in. He had often walked among these trees with me, for hours at a time. Over the years he told me the trees' stories, stories of the relatives who planted them here. Hemma's beech, father's larches. Their wood will burn nicely, I thought. The house's wood stoves were ready for heat.

I had the uneasy feeling it was already too late, that I'd missed everything here as I had everywhere else. This unease gnawed at me during the day and at night and it grew in my dreams like an inner organ displacing the others.

The trees fell during the day, they were sawed down, chopped up and ground into sawdust. I was making good progress. At night the trees returned, in my sleep they grew up round and even inside my house and I got lost among them as I had when a child. The nights here are the worst, even now, as bad as they'd been in my childhood, which was growing back over me, I thought.

From what dreams I woke, into what fears I fell when asleep. This time I left the house and went out for a walk in the garden. I strolled back and forth, lost in thought, and ended up near one of the grounds' darkest corners. Behind a bush I'd not noticed before, I discovered a dead bird, a raven. It lay on its back, wings pressed tight to its sides. The plumage on its breast was torn off. Its chest was plucked bare and its ribcage cut open—a hole, in which I could see its crusted insides.

The raven lay on the ground, eyes closed, as if frozen, although it was summer. When I nudged it with my foot, its eyes opened and once it spotted me it stared at me without blinking. I walked up and down in front of the dead bird, back and forth, always followed by its eyes.

I could hear voices from the house. I was relieved to have company and glad that my absence had been noted. Someone came out of the house and walked up to me and started a conversation, which for some reason they hadn't wanted to have inside in front of the others. I pretended to join in and to listen attentively but all I could think of was how to keep them from seeing the dead bird and lead them off in another direction.

Without knowing why, I was sure that I shouldn't let myself be connected with this creature and so we made our way through the trees and the bushes. My companion was speaking and to assure him I was paying attention, I nodded occasionally but didn't understand a word he was saying. Suddenly, I realized it was Georg who was speaking.

Under another bush, as unfamiliar as the one under which I'd found the first bird, I now saw a second one, also dead, or, rather, *apparently* dead. It lay on its back, wings closed tight with its plumage torn off and a hole in its chest. Its eyes were shut. Just like the other, I thought, as it opened its eyes, fixed them on me intently and did not look away.

I gestured towards the house to draw Georg's attention away from what lay before us but he seemed not to have noticed the bird, even though he had stepped over it. So we went on. The voices grew louder, calling me.

They seemed to be looking for me. I glanced towards the voices and noticed another body and yet another, until I realized that the entire garden was strewn with birds lying on their backs, their eyes all fixed on me. The group of people now came out of the house towards us, talking to me, stepping over the birds without seeming to see them. For them, the birds didn't exist.

Those wounds on the birds' chests, someone had to have caused them, I thought. Georg led the group into the house and I began to search among the bodies and in the undergrowth for evidence of who could have done it. But I found nothing. The number of bird corpses just kept increasing and only then did I realize their bodies were the size of human corpses. After a while, I noticed that the perpetrator lay dead behind the fence, the biggest bird, it must have been he, at least that's what I thought. He lay in the same position as his victims, on his back, his plumage torn off, his eyes closed, and then they opened too and followed me even after I woke.

As a child, I ran on ahead of everything and from everything. I wanted to get away, to get out, to be lost. My goal was always to *escape*.

It worked. I did escape, even from myself. I got away and I'm still gone, away from others and from myself. I'm still running in search of the place I've sought within myself for so long, as I ran from others and from myself. And I've disappeared, no one will find me, not even I, myself.

My personal territory was a spot behind the stove, a place others couldn't fit into. It was mine. There, I crawled into the darkest corner of the room and from there, crouching, hidden, I conducted my surveillance, my first memory, my first retreat. I kept an eye on everything from that spot. I was sheltered from the others' eyes and I missed nothing. The stove was cold, then it warmed up, grew warmer, then hot. Now come out from there, I was told, or things will get hot for you. You won't learn any other way. Finally the stove glowed with heat and the spot was no longer mine.

I want to cut myself off, to withdraw, to escape to a place where I can't be seen but would have a good vantage as I do now here in Landskron. I want to leave it all behind and get away from the past. Here in Landskron, I want to reconnect with myself one more time and go off with myself, by myself, somewhere else.

Was I ever really a child? Was I ever anything but a child? Have I ever been anything but the child I was then, not as they wanted me to be, but the child I nonetheless was?

You're not exactly well liked here but to me that's an advantage. You don't worry what people here think and that I find interesting, the man said to me from his bed, next to which I was sitting. Weeks before I had found a note on the door. *Mr Gärtner next door would welcome a visit.*

You're new here. You seem to be trying this place out and not failing from the beginning. That intrigues me, at least for one visit, I mean. I can't make any promises, you understand. I just wanted to see if you're like all the rest.

I know the people round here and their habits so well, I don't bother leaving my house any more. I haven't left it for years, there's really no point, because I'd just have to come back. Always the same path out of the house, always the same path back home, back to oneself, which is even worse.

My people here are your people, too, or they will be, he said. You'll remember me yet. You see, I get up and read the paper behind drawn curtains. Then, when I open them, the first thing I see is a man who seems to cut himself off from everything round him and apparently with good reason. Every day I see him, how he gathers the branches and leaves that were blown from my tree into his garden during the night. He gathers them up and throws them over the fence. A mama's boy, you see, she stands behind him and points at a twig with her cane. He picks it up and brings it to her like a dog and together they throw it into my yard. Watching things like this is my only contact with the folks round here, so why bother leaving the house? Every day, every morning, I go into the other room and look out of the window at eight-thirty, at twelve-thirty and at three and I watch a woman with her dog. She has the dog shit right in front of that same neighbour's door and he lashes out every time. I hate her, I hate her dog and I hate the neighbour. But most of all, I loathe myself because I can't resist pulling back the curtain to watch the neighbour throw branches over my fence, and because every day at eight-thirty and at twelve-thirty and at three, I look out of the window and watch this woman's dog shit on that neighbour's doorstep. I despise myself for these habits. It's all just sordid. Enough is enough, he said, at least that's what I tell myself every day. I won't leave the house, I'll keep the curtains closed and from now on, I won't leave this room. I won't even get out of bed. I'm going downhill, here in this room, between these walls, in this body. Take a good look.

On the floor above us, I could hear a constant coming and going, the sounds of slamming doors and furniture being moved.

A death, he said when he noticed the noise was distracting me. The man one floor up, he died some time last night. He's still in the house. He's not even cold yet and they're already getting rid of him, as you can hear. It's been going on all afternoon and since last night. They're clearing him out like an animal, his wife, his two sons—friendly people, by the way. Watch out when they're friendly, these people. I'm telling you, you'll remember me yet.

The man is still in the house and his bed is still warm and yet no one has come for him. However, the disembowelling has already begun, this constant back and forth, you can hear it and see it yourself, he said and waved towards the window. It was true. Two young men were carrying rubbish bags filled to bursting out of the house and down to the courtyard, where they threw them into the bins. I'd passed them on my way up the stairs.

In the courtyard, a coffin was shoved into the back of an automobile and it drove away. Standing next to a bin, the men watched it go.

It would have gone the same with me if I hadn't taken care of everything in advance and sold all I had in time or used them up or given them away.

There's nothing to take except my body and I've willed that to the doctors. They've already had a go at it during my lifetime and they can have the damn thing when my time comes. Now and then, someone stops by and checks on me but I'm not cold yet. I signed my body over to them but as for me, myself, they can't have me.

I have nothing, there's nothing left, and so I'm alone. You have to avoid your relatives as much as you avoid yourself. But why am I telling you this? You're a relative, too, a family member who waited for a long time, from a distance, until someone's body began to get cold. You waited for years, Mrs Reger's life was not a short one, God knows. But now she's in Heaven and you are in Landskron.

Your chopping can be heard everywhere. It's a new sound at least. People here like things overgrown, you should know. The wilderness creeps in silently and takes over. This silence, this dead silence in life, Mrs Reger choked on it. Well, you've put an end to it. You've knocked them out of their rigor mortis. Your chopping can be heard everywhere. These people sit in their homes, in the dark, and hear the sound of your chopping, and they think, soon it will be my turn. You're not a friendly person, no one can accuse you of that, and for that we should thank you. Chop the people here right out of their sleep. Maybe one or two will wake up before their night finally falls.

I assume your plan is to clear everything out, everything standing, at least that's what it looks like. You're going to destroy it all, if I'm not mistaken. For now, you still have a lot of work to do with the trees in the wood and also the garden, he said. But I ask myself, what will he do when the wood are all gone and there's not a tree left in the yard? What will he do next? that's what I ask myself, you know. But don't tell me, I want to figure it out on my own. And please, don't stop by again. It's very likely that I would, in fact, ask you in.

My need to be with others is a compulsion. I fall apart, I can't manage without them though they wear me out in the end and always have.

Every conversation I have leaves a stain I can't wash off. The weaker I am—and I've always been weak, it's my only strength—the more avidly some of my acquaintances, my tormentors go after my corpse, the long-dead remains of the nonperson I've become. What a relief it would be, to finally be freed from the burden of my self.

My record of relationships is nothing but a record of wounds, each new meeting just one aberration after another and each new liaison a priori a separation, a disjunction from myself.

I never lost anything in the stories of others, except myself. And so now I'll remain absent. I'll disappear from the outside. I'll withdraw so completely that they'll no longer miss me or if they do, it will be the way you miss someone who died long ago.

I feel a constant compulsion to go to the door and yank it open, just to reassure myself that there isn't, in fact, anyone standing behind it—that kind of reassurance never lasts long. And yet, every time I wake up or when I can't sleep, I reach for the radio in the dark for the voices I simply can't manage without.

My escape was to have no way out, Georg once said. I, too, wanted to wall myself in and to make do alone, without the slightest chance of release. I tried it since then but never could stand it. I would lie my way out or sneak away from it all. I had lots of practice in this and sneaking off was a passion, a passion I still indulge in.

Since coming back to Landskron, I'd finally stopped slipping into habits from my past, at least for a time.

My childhood was a vault, as soundproof as a doctor's consulting room, from which no screams could be heard, no laughter, not a sound could make it out of this vault. At some point I noticed that the door to this cell occasionally stands open for a time. Then I creep out and stand in front of my cell and look in from outside. I walk up and down, back and forth, and I notice that the outer room in which I now stand and which encloses the cage has some room to run, though not much. This room is itself contained within a larger cage and with every opportunity, with every thought of some possibility that seems to open before me like a door leading out of each room, I simply exchange one cell for another. And yet, all the while, I never once manage to escape the cage that I am to myself, not for one second.

Every expectation I set for myself is overshadowed by the judgement, *you can't do it and you never will.* It makes me feel like a child again, alone with that sense of anxiety, as if I'm waiting for someone to come after me, and someone does come after me. It must be my parents, I'd run on ahead of them. I had always run on ahead, as soon as I was able to, so that, for a while, I could be alone and not watched. But I knew they'd catch up because I was compelled to stop and wait for them in that spot as if waiting for a sentence to be passed on me, which then was.

You must know what you're letting yourself in for, Anna had said. I didn't know, how could I? This hell of idleness, I should be doing something else. I'm beginning to miss my work. Outwardly nothing has changed, not a thing, inwardly it's all uneventful, bleak, with vague hopes, concrete fears. The sun rises and sets and I observe myself watching it all.

The rain woke me again. It's the neighbour, I thought, and I was right. He was hammering sheet metal onto the door of the shed which, since I first met him, was no longer my shed.

His car, parked outside the shed, was filled with appliances of every kind. The man's moving in, I thought. If that's true, I'll never get rid of him.

I'm moving out, he said, at least I'm packing my things up for a start. You're not someone I can warm to, that's for sure. You see this, everything's worn out and rusty, ruined by these people. I'm going to have to set up again from scratch but first, all this has to go. Maybe you could help, he said. I did help him because he was moving out, after all, and for that I was grateful enough.

He unscrewed and removed everything he could, which was no small feat. It took hours. We packed it up, drove to his place and unpacked it there, stowing it in his own shed. We rebuilt the workshop there. Each thing went in exactly the same spot it had been in at my place.

We came back and I helped to get rid of my things in this way, finally clearing out everything I'd associated with Landskron until now. I'm chopping down the wood and he's taking the shed off my hands, one carload after another. The place was emptying out and it suited me better all the time.

We worked together without saying a word. It did me good and I was grateful, but it's no way to warm up to someone, I thought.

The shed was completely bare except for a curtain in the far corner. It had already caught my eye. As we worked, a smell had come from the corner, different from that of the shed, and it grew stronger as the room emptied out.

That's probably enough for today, the man said, when I went to pull back the curtain. Tomorrow's another day. This isn't easy for me, you know.

I'd already had the feeling he wanted to get rid of me but I couldn't allow it at this point, not so close to the end of the job. The shed had to be emptied completely, today, right now, I knew, or I'd never be rid of this man. So I pulled back the curtain.

It was a small side room, I now saw. In it was a pole with hooks, hung with skinned hares, the glassy membrane of their sinews shimmered with the colours of flies swarming round them. The pelts were nailed to the adjacent wall. Below the bodies stood a chopping block, snares and traps. The innards, still slightly warm, filled a bucket in the corner. There was no doubt that the man had used the shed as a slaughterhouse.

When had he brought the animals here? When had he butchered them? It must have been at night, which would explain the screams I'd heard, squeals actually, that often woke me with a start.

Your wood, *my* traps, we were a good team, he said, but you're not interested. There were just too many and I had to do something about them. Not any more, though, since you went and cut everything down. It won't be so easy to get lost in your wood now.

Do you like hare? he asked as he took each body off the hook, one after another, and cradled it like a baby before throwing it carelessly on top of the others at the back of his car. I'm guessing you don't.

You're right, I said, now let's go and don't forget anything. We left and found his mother already waiting in front of his reassembled workshop.

You see, I told you he wouldn't have a problem with it, I heard her say as we unloaded the animals. My son is so suspicious, you know. He thinks everything always has to be kept secret.

She took the bodies from me gratefully and her son went into their house.

Just one more word, please, she said when she noticed I too wanted to leave. Death creeps round the house, you understand. With your aunt it was still predictable, but now, it's anyone's guess. I wonder who's next. I've got a bad feeling about Mr Gärtner on the third floor, I have to say. I don't know. His apartment is dark day and night. He doesn't even look out of his window any more. Maybe it doesn't mean anything and we're just anxious, uneasy. I mean, it could be. Until now, after all, he always got up, every day, to air his place but now, I can't bear to think about it, his curtains haven't moved, not for days. A week ago, he flung open his window and began yelling. *I've got a dead man in my house,* he screamed, *and that dead man is me.*

The business with Mr Gruber on the floor above him probably hit a bit too close to home and how could it not. No one is that indifferent. But to carry on like that? *I've got a dead man in my house and that dead man is me.* What can you do? What kind of a person is that? You have to admit, it's not a good time for anyone here on the lake.

Just a few days of silence, not to have to say a single word, not to anyone—that's a paradise I'll never find, not even six feet under.

I almost found it here in Landskron but now, even here, that longing is setting in again, the longing for those few people from my past who are still alive, as if I were tethered to a stake from which I'll never break free, not ever.

I woke up, he said, so at least I knew I wasn't dead. I just wanted to see how long the news would take to reach you for the time when things have, in fact, gone that far.

Mr Gärtner had opened the door and now sat across from me upright on his bed. The curtains were closed. His pictures were propped face-in against the wall, each under the light-coloured spot where it had hung.

I'm preparing for my departure, he said. The truth is I've got myself turned upside down and inside out. I'm turning inwards, going deep within myself, at last. I'm not what you see any more. Or maybe I am. Maybe this way I will finally be recognizable. We'll see.

I've always lived in the shadows, he said. Like Mr Reger, I prefer to live in obscurity, and like him, I lived the life of a dead man. Compared with him, I had it easy. But not any more, not since he's gone, I mean.

I once was somebody, as Mr Reger was, too. We both did something or didn't, depending on your point of view, and neither of us ever came to terms with it.

There's no air, no air, no air at all—I often can't breathe at night now, you understand, but it will get better, I think, it's not over yet. And if it is, then the swallows can fly south without me.

My entire life I've kept others at a distance. Only now am I finally beginning to miss them. That's how I know I've reached the final round. And now to sleep, just sleep, be done and gone. But first, I have to do one more thing and for that I need you. So be warned.

Georg wanted to tell you something but never managed to do it. So now *I* will try to tell you something and maybe, eventually, you'll understand.

You're definitely not a good person, he said, and you make no pretence of being one. I respect that. People don't open up to you very easily, at least they don't seem to. And since you don't try to win them over either, maybe we can talk. I assume you haven't come here out of pity. I hate pity of any kind, it's just another form of contempt.

So now I've put myself on trial, maybe it's my way of answering for myself. We'll see. I will testify against myself, I will tell you, if I can tell anyone at all.

Mr Gärtner hadn't taken his eyes off me the entire time and only now did I notice the spots of livor mortis on his face. His arms, too, were laced with blotches. Death had painted its mark on his face, which he eagerly held towards me.

My doctor is dead, just imagine, he said when he noticed my alarm. They spend their lives signing death sentences. When the time comes they sign their own sentences and finally leave others in peace.

In real life other people die—Georg, Mrs Reger, the man on the floor above. But in my dreams, it's only ever I who die, he said. It's been that way since the war.

What about my shoes, which ones should I wear to my grave? That's what's on my mind these days. I'm preparing myself, you understand, but still, I, myself, am just a formality. From the beginning, I've always made excuses and detours. For my entire life, I've kept a distance from myself and with good reason. I would never have wanted to have anything to do with someone like me, believe me.

Georg wanted to tell you something. You were the only one he trusted enough and I respect you for that. But still, presumed intimacy is the worst, so be on your guard. It would be better if you turned away, he said, even better if you left right now. If I'm ever back among the living, I'll come to see you. On the other hand, maybe not, he said, you might as well stay. If I did come back, I'd probably still be unable to connect to you.

These urges that come over me now, they are urges I've always felt, like the urge to yell out of the window, *I've got a dead man in my house and that dead man is me.* I assume you heard about it. These people, they think they've defeated you just because you've spared them.

I really do have a dead man in my house, in my head, actually, under my skin, in my memory. That's where he's buried and that's where I've visited him all these years.

Dying brings people together. Killing draws you even closer. Georg and I became very close to someone this way and I've lived with that all these years, you understand.

If you have a conscience, you'll fall into it, I always told Georg. He fell into the pit. I didn't. He never got over it. He felt he was being haunted and he was, always. But not I. For me, it only began once Georg was gone. He can't tell anyone anything now. So I'm bringing charges against myself, in his place, by beginning to tell you about it, if I may.

What we've become is horrifying and what we will become is disastrous. We're destroyed from the beginning, from birth, annihilated. We slip out of one body and spend the rest of our lives wishing we could get into another, in vain. We waste away because of it. But it's a mistake to believe it will end with our death, that it will be over and done with for good. Dying doesn't solve anything. It's over and done with, at least, but it's never made good, not ever.

We look each other in the eye but we're already mistaken, he said after a pause during which he grew more and more restless.

I can feel it all beginning again, he said. I'm already trying to hide. I'm withdrawing from everyone, even you, though in truth I'm trying to get away from myself. The reason I want to elude you is that I intend to give myself up and with that surrender to finally escape from myself. But I keep putting it off, you see how I'm hedging. It's still too soon, he said. We slip out of our mothers and are dead, but it doesn't stop with that death. That's just the beginning. We die of our parents as of some illness. First we die of our fathers and our mothers. Then we die of our husbands and wives. Then we die of our children, but in the end and in all, it's really just our own selves that kill us off.

Refuge, he said, fear. I've spent my life looking for refuge. I've sought refuge in others, I've sought it everywhere and all I ever found was myself. Rejection, disgust. Never a sense of relief, only a constant feeling of suffocation. But for years now, you understand, he said, I've been terrified that someone might have turned to me for refuge.

And I, should I say yes? Have I said yes, have I even once ever said the word *yes* to anyone? And if I have, did I really mean it?

Absence makes others bearable, the woman in the graveyard said to me. I had gone looking for her, Section IV, Row 9, Bench 2. That's where she sat, and she greeted me like an old acquaintance.

My husband, ever since he passed, I've grown closer to him, she said, whether I like it or not. He'll be there waiting for me, he always said, no matter how long it takes. I'll wait for you, he said as his time drew nearer, you see, and so he draws me back to him.

Until you join me, I'll lie alone in the ground, he always said to me, there's not much choice, so I'll wait for you. We'll have time for each other then and you'll certainly have me. Well, he can certainly wait for me. I won't follow him, not by choice, not again. He'll have me for long enough then.

We seek refuge but come upon fear, he said, and you, too, you're seeking refuge but only find your own fear. Mr Gärtner knew me well.

I want to be my own foundation, in everything, you understand, and to dig up anything anyone else might ever have wreaked upon me, I dig and I dig, yet all I ever find is evidence of what I've done to myself.

I turned away from myself, he said, that's how it all began. I opened my eyes with my first cry and have looked round me since then, but I've only looked outward, away from myself, avoiding myself in this way, I never had eyes to look into myself.

And now, I'm turning again, I'm turning inward, in fact. I'm closing the curtains, I'm closing my eyes and looking deep into myself, I had a late start, there's not much time left, but I'm finally faced with myself. It's grim, he said. I look in the mirror and see that I'm facing a dead man.

Come join me in my fear, there's room enough for two. Look into my heart, you'll still only find yourself. It's all a mistake. You come into the world by mistake, to the wrong parents, into the wrong surroundings, an error, the next one. Your entire life you are taken for someone you're not, someone you should be but definitely are not.

Over and over again, from the beginning and without end, the same feeling, what's happening to me, why can't I escape from this place, without end, and again from the beginning to the brink of exhaustion that never finally comes.

Life is good beneath the ground, my father had said when his father's coffin was lowered into the earth, it's like living with others, you are with your own and that's good.

Back then the child I was lay down on the ground in that very spot, I had loved my grandfather and I lay down with him, in the earth, in the grave, and they let me lie there.

Life is good beneath the ground and yet a grave is the wrong place to look for Heaven, I heard my father say as the earth was already piling up on top of me.

Is the wrong place, I heard and I knew it was *my* place. No one would look here, not for me, they would not find me here, and it was true, no one ever looked for me there.

Back then, I hid myself for good, even from myself.

Ever since I haunt graveyards in my dreams. Since then I wander, lost among graves, in search of the grave in which I lie and which is nowhere to be found.

Night has fallen and I know that soon they'll come searching. They will search for my grave and will dig to make room for one of their own, one who will come later, then they'll open the grave and they'll find me in it, so I have to get out. I have only a night, a few hours, then they will come and they'll dig. I dig and I dig, I don't stop digging and I stand below in the grave, in the pit, and can't find myself or my grandfather, it's always the same, and yet, I can feel down there that it's the right place, this is *my* place, I realize then, and I realize the child I was is already gone. They can come and look and dig, they can all come after me, all of them together, there is nothing to find, not this time, not now and not tomorrow either, never, and I'll be awake and alert and I'll stand on two feet and will fall into the new day as into a noose.

I drew the curtain aside so I could see into the courtyard. Twelve-thirty, Mr Gärtner said, the stories about me are increasing. I lie here in bed and watch as I'm fed to the rumour mill, take a look down there and admit it, they've already begun pointing at us up here.

They come every day now, in my dreams, they come to take me away, during the day they come to check on me, to see if the time has come and in my dreams they come to get me. Well, let them come. Until now I've always chased them away.

And then I wake up and I'm not on my way after all and won't be for some time yet. I've told you it could take a while and it's good that it will, I don't want something for nothing.

The room was empty except for the bed and the chair on which I was sitting.

I'm clearing out my apartment, he said, to finally clear myself out too, I already began the process, excavations of all kinds, you understand, I dig and I dig. From outside, it looks bare, but as for me, inside I'm full, I'm bloated to bursting with everything you stuff inside yourself over the course of a life, what you hoard and then can't get rid of, only to choke on in the end.

There are people who've destroyed you. There are people to whom you owe your existence. There are people who've been killing you. There are people who helped make you what you are. How pitiful they are, in truth, those who tore you down back when you were at their mercy, and when you think how much power you've granted them in the years since then, simply because you still suffer because of them though, in fact, they've long since disappeared, they're no longer here. They've vanished from the face of the earth and into the earth, yet under the ground they proliferate, they flourish like mushrooms inside you, they've disappeared from the face of the earth but not from your head. They haven't been able to escape your thoughts, you still hold them captive and so they still control you and they always will.

There's only one way to escape them, to get out from under their sway—because you play a part in your own destruction, I, at least, did. I was instrumental, I joined in whenever I could, time and again I played the victim by driving my own destruction—the only way to get free in such a case is to turn against yourself, and for me, things were always this way, not once were they any different. I joined in, he said, time and again, in many things, in everything, actually, always, always and again, during the war, before the war and after it too, for as long as I can remember, in my case it was so.

You must turn against yourself, ruthlessly. I was never quite up to it, too much of a coward, you see.

Now, I'm turning against myself at last, a little late perhaps, much too late in fact, but still, what others haven't managed to do to us, we have to do to ourselves and in this way finally take responsibility for ourselves, continuously, definitively, again and again, always beginning anew, until we finally understand who we are, where we stand, and we keep on with it ceaselessly, constantly, without interruption, until it finally has an effect.

A long line of cars crawled by in front of the house, honking loudly. They wouldn't stop honking, a wedding convoy, I thought.

The wedding guests, he laughed as the honking reached him, future funeral guests. The rays from the sun of divorce can't pierce the wedding clouds, not yet, they beget and they propagate, they become parents and die off.

We look for a homeland in another but can't find it, yet we still don't stop searching. We go from one person to the next, searching for a homeland and not finding one, there's always one person who seems to be it, this time and now, this time and now and for ever, but still we don't find a homeland because there is none to be found, not in others and not in ourselves, he said, because there is, in truth, no such thing. We search for a home and don't find it, then we finally stop searching, we give up, our desire to find it eventually runs out, at least outwardly, outwardly we give up and begin searching in ourselves, we burrow and poke round deep in ourselves, as we'd only done in others until then, we search through our childhoods and don't find it, how could we, childhood has never been a homeland, still we keep searching and we get lost, we go back and forth, we examine our past selves at each particular age and still find no home, then we stop searching, even within, and we grow older, we grow old and still can't find it because there is none to find, not ever. But the truth is, we don't really give up. We replace the object of our desire with the search itself, we replace the idea of homeland, which doesn't exist, with longing itself, with the craving we have for home, merely to have something to hold on to, an illusion, a delusion from the beginning. We search for ourselves and each other in vain, we leech on to each other with our bodies, we creep into each other and then slip out again, but never truly reach each other, or worse, the biggest delusion of all, we believe we once actually reached someone else or that we even simply were close.

I lay on my back in the reeds, under water. People stood along the shore, looking down at me and poking at the reeds with their poles. I lay before them in the water and they didn't see me or else I wasn't the one they were looking for, so I drifted past them.

The waves lapped gently at my body. Long strands of hair hung down from the reeds, from the stalks, and brushed over my face. The current pulled me slowly along the shore under the trees. Hair hung down into the lake from the willows as well.

I had gone some distance from the people, I now realized, so I crawled onto the shore and lay down on the ground in the grass, which I clung to as if I were hanging onto a cliff face, until I noticed that it wasn't grass in my hands, it was hair. The entire ground, the grass, was a field of human hair.

I lay without moving until finally I opened my eyes and saw something move in the ground not far from me, a slight bulging, a swelling that expanded and contracted, it rose in front of me, then sank again, only to reappear in another location. The ground threw up mounds of dirt that moved slowly, alone or in groups, they swelled up from the earth as if from its skin and churned as if bodies were stirring beneath it. These mounds expanded, they grew larger and longer and were soon the size of a human body. They slowly inched away from me, like caterpillars, then returned to the spot from which they had risen.

The turmoil in the ground increased, growing stronger and more frequent. There were many mounds now, they swelled and sank, disappearing again into the ground, they moved in waves towards one spot and clustered there in a mound that throbbed and twitched, the entire ground was in motion, new mounds constantly appeared and moved towards the rest.

The people I had seen earlier on the shore came over to the mounds and now walked among them, their poles had become brushes, combs, actually, with which they began stroking the mounds as they knelt beside them; these mounds of hair that expanded and contracted seemed to writhe under their touch.

They were all bald, naked and bald, I now noticed. I put my hands to my head and realized that I, too, had no hair. I was naked and bald just like them.

They knelt beside their mounds and drew their combs along the surfaces and followed them to where the other mounds had clustered. They stroked the gathered mounds with their brushes and the pile grew smaller, the movement under the earth's surface changed direction, the bodies drew apart and sank back into the ground, the pile shrank even more and the seething abated and the earth quieted down, became as smooth and as flat as it had been before.

We always think we've left hell behind, only to realize that we've only begun heading towards it. They came today, first in a dream and then in real life, this time they were stronger, this time they took me and I went on a trip, finally. Mr Gärtner welcomed me into his room on the second floor of the hospital in Hermagor as if into his home.

First it was Villach, I wasn't right for that place, *there's no room for someone like you*, they said, so we kept going, but they don't want me here either, *condition too advanced*, so this is simply a stopover, the final destination is Laas, he said, I haven't arrived yet, my arrivals have always been departures. In Hermagor it's getting dark, in Laas night will fall; there, the elderly lose their way in the forest. In Hermagor there's still hope but no one returns from Laas. But I haven't gotten to that point yet, I'm not there yet, dying makes you lively, it revives you once more.

He sat before me in bed and ran his hands along the tubes that grew out of and into his body.

It's all loss, he said, you get to know someone and then you part ways. In the best case we lose each other, we can't expect more, not ever, it's one giant contradiction, and yet, we don't have a choice.

Until now I'd never felt at home with myself and yet I'm finding myself here and now and in this way, I'm finding my bearings, facing up to myself. Facing up to myself, without judgement, could be a beginning, I believe, or it could be an ending, or at least the beginning of the end of my past, of my story.

But still. There's always the fear it will surface, even here. Here, I swallow down sleep, it flows through these tubes, there's no defence against it and I no longer know what I'm saying.

People are constantly asking me questions. They want to know everything but they won't hear a thing, not from me. That, they can't handle. So they send me to Laas. Dead of his own inner silence, they'd say.

It's no different the other way round, they never say anything about me, he said, except that I'll soon feel *much better* in Laas. You can't trust them. Go to the window and take a look outside for me. I want to know where I am in case they're trying to trick me. We're not in Laas, are we now? We're definitely in Hermagor, tell me where we are, I insist.

I'd already been staring out of the window all the while. I'd noticed a dragonfly larva on the windowsill and it was beginning to move. I drew near to watch its actions more closely.

The insect had already eaten through the casing round its head and it crawled out like a worm and began gnawing on the shell, it dragged its entire length out, the skin of its wings was wrapped round its body. Its wings were wet and slippery and soft and they unfolded as I watched. They dried in the breeze, blood surged through the veins and as the skin of the wings dried in the sun, they began to shimmer, becoming glassy and stiff as the wrinkles smoothed out. Colours emerged on the insect's body, growing luminous and bright. Now the insect stretched out its wings and kept them spread out in the air, then began to flutter them, but still they kept buckling. The breeze lifted it up and forced it back to the ground and up against the windowpane once more. Again and again it returned to the casing from which it had crawled.

It rose in the air but always returned to the same spot. Each time the distance it covered was greater.

I opened the inner pane of the window to touch the casing it had left behind. At that moment, the dragonfly returned and landed on my finger, gripping it tightly. I brought it into the room and sat down on the chair.

Mr Gärtner lay in the bed with his tubes—they hung from him limply—a discarded marionette.

The ties that bind us become ever more constricting, he said when he guessed what I was thinking. All our lives, we hang from them as if from a rope, we cannot get free. They shouldn't have cut me free at birth, that's when it all began.

And now in Laas, they'll hang me out to dry, I don't need to go there, you understand, I don't want to go to Laas.

Then should we unplug you now? I asked. You should probably let me know if that's what you want.

The longing, he said after a pause, the urge to lie on the ground once more, out in the open, arms spread wide and legs stretched out.

These days, the nights, the dreams from which there's no waking, always the same, I see in the dreams how they bend over me and say, it'll get better, everything will be fine, he'll pull through, they lean over me and lift me and bend me forwards and back. There are lots of them, I lie on the ground before them, beneath them, someone has stretched out my legs and my arms too, I see them kneel over me, they're screaming, now they're slapping my face, someone yanks my head upwards, Mr Weber, can you hear me, open your eyes, listen to me, he can't hear anything, I open my eyes wide, I stare at them and I see that my eyes are still shut, open his eyes for him, I hear, they're not going to open on their own, it burns, he won't be opening them any more, one of them kneels on top of me, takes my head in his hands and wipes my forehead, brushing my eyes as he does, they open and he shines a light in them, nothing there, he's passing, you know, we're losing him, now the burning, my eyes are wide open, he's gone all stiff, stiff and rigid, I hear them say, he's gone, but that isn't true, I'm not gone yet, I'm here, I say, but they can't hear me, I close my eyes and see that they're still wide open, in that case they're right, they blow air into my lungs, they pump me full of air, I become weightless and float in the air, but not any more, I slam back onto the ground, we can't hold him, he's passing, he's leaving us, I'm back on the floor, I feel weightless again and my body slams down, he's a goner, but that isn't true, I'm not gone yet, I'm here, I scream and raise my hand, but they don't notice and I see that my hand is still on the floor next to me, my legs are still splayed, my arms, too, so it's true, they must be right, I close my eyes but they're still wide open, someone closes them for me, not yet, don't close his eyes yet, I hear, think of the woman, which woman, it's Vera who bends over me, open his eyes, my eyes are opened and I can see, they're blowing air into my lungs, they're pressing down and pumping me up, now the burning, I feel weightless again, he's coming round, he's coming, I hear, we got him back after all, his heart's going again, it's not over yet, it's going to work out, you have to be strong now, Mrs Weber, we've got him now, we got him back, then why doesn't he speak, she says then, I'm lying on the ground in front of them, no longer floating, they've got me now, I'm here, it's all going to be fine, it's not over yet, he made it, he really did make it, then why won't he speak, she screams then, his heart is still working, he will be fine, someone tells her, someone found him, the neighbour's boy discovered him, I hear, cut him down, a child, but that isn't true, they shine a light in my eyes, he's slipping again, I hear, all stiff, maybe I'll escape them after all, I don't want to but still do, he's going, I don't want to but still do, they can't reach me, and I'm weightless again, the burning is gone, this time it won't work, I hear, it's pointless, and I feel heavy again, there before them, he's done for, he's finished, it's over, I hear, they bend down towards me and lift me, where are they taking me, to a small room, they lay me down, I lie there, he really did it, I lie there before them, it's not true even though that's what they're saying, there's no point in telling them since they can't hear me, I leave my body to their lies, he's gone now, for good, I see them lay me down and leave me lying there, someone has folded my hands, they straighten up, they stand up straight and they leave, I lie there, I stay behind, someone comes and closes my eyes, where is Vera, now I'm alone, this silence, so it's come to this, but that isn't true, I see them returning to me in this room, I see that they're washing my body, they're washing me now, the face that bends over me is familiar, a nurse who had also bent over Grandfather, when his time came, she had washed Grandfather's body in just this way, so I must be in Laas, this is Laas, I look at the nurse's face, the view through the window, the fields, the village, this is Laas, so the time has come, we all end up in Laas at some point or other, each in his own time, from here there is no return, I visited Georg here, Anton died here and Karl, Grandfather was the last, life ended here for him too, these hands washed Grandfather's body as well, they're familiar to me but still strange, the face that bends over me, smiling down at me as if I were an infant, is *my* nurse, I see, she isn't alone, there are lots of them, standing, surrounding my bed, bending over me, smiling down at my body, now they're all here, my relatives' faces, the ones I tried to escape my entire life, now they're all here, standing here by my bed, they've come because of me, now I'm the one who needs company, they're visiting me now, I draw back, I close my eyes and pretend I'm asleep, I sleep and I watch them through closed eyelids, they cannot escape me, this too will pass, I hear them say, why did you do this, tell me, my eyes are shut but their words can't escape me, they stand next to me, their words sail past and beyond me, it was bound to happen, we knew it all along, a life like that could never have come to any good, and how calm he looks now, how peaceful, never this peaceful before, you can hardly recognize him, he's out of the wood now, it's all behind him, their phrases are familiar, I myself stood at bedsides in Laas often enough, and now with my eyes closed I see them standing before me in their finery, as always in Laas, all dressed up, in their malice they stand before me, talking past me and at me, and with their talk and their silence, they smooth everything over, they come to terms with each other, I think and I retreat from them even further, still I cannot escape from their words, is he sleeping or does he just look like it, it was a child, apparently, who found him, imagine, a child, how horrible, just as with Paul, I pretend I'm asleep, I sleep and I listen, they talk me to death, not even the quietest syllable escapes me, they smile and with their talk and their silence they smooth everything over, they come to terms with each other, I think, that's always what happens in Laas, I lie in my bed before them, inaccessible, I'm lying in state, they stare down at me and smile and dare to touch me, they stroke me gently with flowers, my parents stand off to the side, they cope with it all, they find explanations, explain it away, there's not much to say, they know it all already and have always known and so they say nothing, they are silent and smile, this, too, will pass, things will get better, I think, they were there and are here and they sought me out, they plagued me, they saw me one more time, they had another to watch in his death throes, it revives them, always has, they'll feed on this for a while, they saw me once more, so now they'll leave, at some point they go, they are gone, and I stay behind, I'm finally alone, I leave my story to their lies and I stay behind, alone, they are gone.

After a night without dreams, I woke suddenly, I dreamt, and I got up and found my bearings, then noticed that at some point the music had stopped. I'd just begun fiddling with the radio when a drop fell from the ceiling onto my forehead.

I went over to the basin and stood before the mirror. By the time I got there, my head was completely soaked. It was clear that the house had begun to fight back. Water was streaming from the ceiling. I ran into the hallway, calling for Vera. The hallway and the landing were flooded as well, water streamed down the stairs, I run up the stairs and call for Vera and I wade down the hallway to her door, which stands open, I enter her room and see an old woman sitting there. I don't know her or maybe I do, I can't tell, she sits in a chair with a blanket on her lap and her hands folded upon it. She smiles as if she's been expecting me and says, don't be afraid, it's raining, which was true, but only inside, outside there's no rain.

We're safe in this room, she said, and this, too, was true, the room was intact, completely dry, but this was not reassuring.

With a friendly nod, she motioned me closer, and so I stood near her but still kept my distance.

She ran her hands slowly through her hair, then tore it from her head and held it out towards me. She was completely bald. I moved back a few steps. She held the wig out towards me like a gift for a long time. When she realized I wouldn't take it, she pulled a comb out from under the blanket on her lap and began combing the wig.

Whose hair was this? That's what I've been wondering all these years, she said as if to herself, whose hair am I wearing, who is it I am combing when I comb myself, who am I really, anyway?

When I woke it was clear that my situation was not good. I've got someone in my house, going in and out of my home, someone I don't know, this woman comes into my house each day, walks past me, climbs the stairs to her room and holes herself up in there and doesn't come out again until evening, then she creeps out and leaves. This has been going on for months.

She didn't lock the door behind her this time and I went in. The woman stood by the window, looking out at the lake and completely ignored me. She simply took no notice of me.

Suddenly, someone enters a room, she said without turning round, someone suddenly enters a room and is there and the room is never the same again, and what was once your space will never be yours again, just as you will never be the same person again, do you know how that is? she asked. No, you don't, and why should you?

I've been expecting you, I've waited and waited, it was a question of time, I knew, until you came and took me away from here.

But Truth is shy, it doesn't let itself be fed, it doesn't eat from just anyone's hand. But still, you've tried, and with patience, and I've fed on that patience. Now here you are and you want to know what took place.

The day before I'd cut down a stand of young birches. She had watched me from her window.

You're chopping down the trees, she said, digging up the flowers, that's good. Flowers are always a sign of guilty conscience. They decorate their graves with flowers; if you go by the flowers, Landskron is one giant graveyard.

Those birches, she said, they always make you think of forests and of people running through them, naked people being herded through the trees to one place.

She turned and looked me directly in the eye, as if to signal that our conversation was finished, and it was, for a time. I was on my way out, my hand already on the doorknob, when she called me back into the room.

It happened a long time ago, she said. How it all began, no one knows. In any case it ended here, in this room and with me.

Victims never get away from the scene of the crime, they themselves are the crime scene, they seek it out, again and again, they keep returning, they never get free.

Sometimes I remember. Sometimes I don't. It's different each time, you can't access your own past after a while, I tried, the early years, the vivid images, you're not alone then. Here in the present, I track our past selves, Ludwig's and mine, here in the present I return to the paths we shared and still I can't reach us, I lose sight of the two of us every time.

She was holding a letter, I saw. Letters were spread out on the desk as well. Aside from these letters nothing in the room had been changed.

I looked at the desk. Yes, I write letters here, she said after a pause, although I won't send a single one. No one will release me any time soon from the guilt others bear towards me; as for my guilt, there is no address for that.

Any time you survive, you pay for your survival with your conscience and with loss. I survived in this house, in this room, but not in myself. They didn't take me, you see, and I didn't go with him.

Even without taking the slightest risk it was easy to lose everything and that's what I did. I took no risks but still I lost everything. I didn't go with him, you see.

They took a part of me back then and I never got it back. I disappeared somewhere then, I disappeared into the absence of someone and in that absence, I was lost.

Ludwig. He died because of me, you understand, he died instead of me and I survived in his stead.

My life changed for ever back then and now it goes on without me, without him.

She walked past me and sat down at the desk, opening and closing the drawers as if she wanted to open them for me, then finally got up again and stood stiffly in front of me.

Things between us were weakening, she said, even then. We didn't realize at the time but it was true. Diminished, dried out, things had stalled at some point as time passed and our relationship was dying. But not for me, she said, never for me. Things then were just as they are now, exactly the same, intimacy, longing and desire, hope and fear, turning away and leaving.

It's a mistake to believe we can possess each other, this delusion does us in and yet it's what I lived for, she said. This delusion is all we have really, all we've had from the beginning and still have, and we long for it, our longing for this delusion is not small and can easily fill a lifetime.

You get close to another person and pass through a new landscape, coming from another landscape into which you'd retreated long before and suddenly everything changes. Coming from one story, you pass into another, into your own story with another person, someone you once were close to, here in this region, very close, and now, your intimacy with this person strikes you as an actual or an apparent mental and emotional delusion and it expands, engulfs, subsumes you completely, just as it had when you'd become consumed with that other person and with yourself and with each other, completely and utterly consumed, and from that moment on, you had eyes and ears only for him. On my way here each day, I follow winding roads over mountains and through forests, and after kilometres, I finally pass a house, it's no refuge, the isolated farms, each suicide only a stone's throw from the next, each house a source of distrust, you picture the beams in each barn, and from each beam hangs a corpse, each and every place is the site of a failure to connect, the memory of such failures at any rate.

The names of those places, she said, Inner Desolation, Outer Desolation, Desolation. The names of the living, the names of the dead, the living bear the names of the dead, here as everywhere else, they wear them out and pass them on and everything remains the same.

And then I come here, to this place, and everything changes. There are no corpses hanging from the barn beams and the trees are no longer bare but lush and bursting with sap, she said, and so I come to this place, I arrive in Landskron, in this house, and all I hear is the beat of my own thoughts about the past and about the man I cherished and honoured and loved then and have loved ever since. He's always there in my head, in my every thought and again I realize what I've always known and have been unable to escape since then, that I still love this person, I never stopped loving him, in truth, I can't live without him, although I have, I had to and I did, I had no choice, and I realize that I can't live in a place so full of my past with him, even though I have and I've never felt anything here but his absence.

This place has held nothing but absence since then and it always will, the lake and the boats floating on it, the driftwood, the buoys, the reeds, it's all only memory, everything's gone, the houses on the opposite shore, the space between the houses where we once walked and that mountain on which the houses are built and from which we will never again look out over it all together.

Mr Gärtner lay on the ground, out in the open, arms spread wide and legs stretched out.

I was still able to escape them this time, but Hermagor, stay away from Hermagor, he said, at least I managed to escape them one more time.

I'm not deluding myself, my way into the ground leads past the doctors and they're already standing as my honour guard. My doctor in Landskron who died recently—I've mentioned him before—each time he put a patient in the ground, he weeded his garden meticulously afterwards. And you knew it would keep him busy for weeks, it was certain, dependable, you could count on it, you understand, you could set your watch by it.

But the customs in Hermagor now are new and that's frightening.

Would you like to go home, Mr Gärtner? one doctor asked me today. *Just think it over, should I send you home, Mr Gärtner? Is that what you want?*

Of course, I want to go home, right now, I told him, at least at home I'll die simply of being myself.

It's your heart, he said, *your heart will kill you. You know, its beating wakes you your whole life and then one day its beating does you in. It keeps you alive your entire life, but then, in the end, it brings your death.*

He grabbed his lower back as if he were in pain. This reversal in the sense of being healthy, he said. When young, you occasionally felt unwell but with the years this sense of illness becomes the norm and in the end you only feel well unexpectedly and only for the length of a breath. Before, you objected to this feeling of sickness and now you react against these moments of well-being.

Today, in a dream or in reality, I can't remember which, he said, I was in a panic because I woke to the sound of prayer and the prayer was for me.

You've got to stay out of Hermagor. They ride rough-shod over you there, as if you weren't already half-dead, always with a good-natured smile on their lips, which in truth expresses nothing but contempt, they extract gratitude from you, like everyone else. Helplessness, gratitude, there you very quickly learn both, you know.

Life in Hermagor lasts a few months, they don't allot you more than that, a few days, maybe weeks, and the prospect of Laas.

And all that doesn't grow stronger with age, everything that has made you what you are, it all becomes more exaggerated, every virtue, every vice, the lot; in my case it's cowardice and fear. Guile, actually, was always one of my main traits.

But why am I telling you this, you're cunning as well, you've seen it all already. Everything grows stronger, he said, becomes more pronounced, more forceful and distinct, insofar as it can, as do dishonesty—everything, in truth—debts, indebtedness, because now everyone I've ever owed something to is dead, they all died off before I had a chance to get closer to them.

So beware, he said, closeness requires distance and that you don't have, distance yourself from me and later, we'll no doubt be happy that we didn't have much to do with each other.

It was too late for distance, I knew perfectly well, this man had burrowed his way through to me and perpetuated his work in me. I'd already become close to him. I'd visited him in Hermagor and was taking him out of there now. They had telephoned and said that Mr Gärtner should be picked up, he had given up on himself and was right to, his case was hopeless, a few days, a matter of weeks, a month at the most, that would be the end of Mr Gärtner, it will all be over for him soon, please come quickly, and I came and took him out, away from Hermagor and brought him back with me to Landskron.

What did they tell you? he asked. how long do I have? It was summer, the weather was hot and the car window open. On the back seat the days fluttered in my diary. I closed the window and said nothing.

On the way, we passed an abandoned quarry and despite his weak condition, he insisted on showing it to me and leading me through the grounds.

A crater blasted into the landscape, surrounded by wood, a wall in which swifts and swallows had built their nests, a constant coming and going, solitary pines twisted out of the rock, a quarry like any other.

He lay on the ground before me in the sparse grass and stared up at the rock face for a long time without saying a word.

I always loved this place, he said, Georg did too. We both liked this place, we liked quarries in general but especially this one.

The forest is gradually reclaiming these rocks, it's trying but hasn't managed to yet, which is good. Devastation should remain devastation, otherwise no one can recognize it.

You hear of someone's divorce and you want one too. You hear someone committed suicide and you want to kill yourself too, that very minute. We hear that someone's got divorced, want to as well and yet we don't do it. We hear of a suicide and want to kill ourselves too but we don't do it, we don't do it on our own even though the time is always right.

Some do, he said, some do after all and at some point have enough courage, despair and clarity to actually see it through.

I tried once myself, in this quarry, on this cliff face, the one time I was clear-headed enough. After Paul's suicide, it seemed that my time, too, had come.

No one expected it of Paul, it had never occurred to any of us, not once. And yet, he did. He got my respect and gave me courage, and with this borrowed courage, I came here, to the quarry, climbed up onto this cliff but then just climbed down to the ground out of cowardice. I lacked Paul's clarity, quite simply, and not only I. Georg didn't have it either. Georg came and got me down from this cliff, just as you came and got me from Hermagor today.

This sudden inability to die, this decision not to die, to not want to die, not then, not there and not since then either, not now, nor in Hermagor, and so on and so forth, he said. The only consolation is that it will happen at some point without any effort on my part. I will be able to count on my own heart some day.

I didn't have enough courage to fly, Georg came and got me down from the cliff, lured me down, actually. He knew he'd have been next, after Paul and after me, it would have been his turn, that much he knew. When he got me off the cliff, he was getting himself off it too. We'd survived here once already, several years earlier, we hid here when they were searching for someone else and found him.

I looked out of the window and saw that everything was just as it had been in a dream I remembered. It was late afternoon, early autumn, even the woman in the half-open bay window across the way, who had been watching me in my dream, was still there and had apparently not lost interest in me.

It's a dream, I thought and I lowered myself onto the bed to keep dreaming it but everything remained exactly the same.

Sheets were draped over everything in the room, I noticed, and the walls were bare, as if it had been abandoned long ago.

I sat down at the desk on which were strewn letters and pieces of paper covered with notes in an unfamiliar handwriting. I picked several sheets at random from the clutter and the sentences on them seemed to have been written just as randomly—illegible passages in which someone seemed to be defending or justifying himself for something I couldn't make out. Some of them were haunting, as if they could reveal what had happened. But they gave nothing away.

Then I was also struck by an odour that I hadn't noticed before, even though it was strong, penetrating, a kind of medicinal odour, the smell of the elderly, the odour of Landskron, my odour, and the courtyard in front of the house was actually the lake, I now saw, and the room I was in, my room, the one that used to be Ludwig's room, which I'd given to the woman who was watching me from my own bay window and hadn't stopped watching me from the very room I sat in, not even for a moment. I remembered that at our last meeting, this table had been covered with the same sort of letters and notes.

The letters were sealed but not addressed and I didn't dare open them, only when I held them up to the light, could I make anything out through the envelope.

Let them come, one said. *They can come for me. They won't find me.*

These sentences offered no answers, at least not at the moment. That woke me. I went to the room. There wasn't a single piece of paper on the desk.

Ludwig's boat, my boat, our shared delusion back then, the woman said as she sat in the boat with me, combing her fingers through the water.

Sleeplessness had been driving me out on the lake every night for some time. After midnight, I would row out, pull up the rudder and drift with the current until daybreak.

I had just returned from one of these outings and was tying the boat up to one of the posts of the dock when she climbed into my boat and asked me to take her back out on the water. We rowed across the lake and along the opposite shore, not saying anything for a long time.

Ludwig's not dead, she said, he survived. I mourned for him as if he were dead but I'm the one who died. I only realized this after a time. We didn't decide on each other, so we decided against ourselves. All the same, we spared each other that way.

Then I remembered having seen the name *Inge* on the side of the boat. It had been painted over but was still faintly visible.

Georg died in this boat, I said into the silence after a pause.

Knowing what has broken you can offer a foothold, she said. At least he had that. I can live with Georg's death.

As we passed a buoy, she suddenly reached into the water and held on to it tightly.

With Ludwig, it was a happy time, she said. We could close our eyes and believe we weren't alone.

The shock of having one's dreams come true, you know that feeling. It never quite came to that but we were close. I was never interested in what I could have. The unattainable, the impossible, that's what I always found alluring and I still do, the only thing for me that didn't eventually die off or wasn't dead from the beginning. The most important events in my life have always been those that never happened.

The lake was quieter than I'd ever experienced it; you could hear the slightest noise even deep in the gardens onshore. An apple fell from a tree and I thought of Vera.

That sudden shortness of breath, she said, airless rooms, you know what I mean, unpredictable, a collapse, actually, fear.

Ludwig was gone, often, and often for years, but he always returned from these absences. Not actually, she said, he never actually moved physically. But he comes to me, in my head. A cause seeks its effect.

We had returned to our shore of the lake. Bells rang in the distance.

We're rowing over a sunken city, she said. According to the legend, a wind blows under water. Whenever the lake takes someone, the bells announce the dead's arrival.

A few gardens further on, we came to the source of another sound. A lawnmower had eaten its way into the dirt. A body lay next to it without moving. After a time, a young man came out of the house. The man's son, she said. He went up to the lifeless body, bent down and spoke to it. From the boat we could see an ambulance stop at the gate to the property. We could see the man's neighbours as well, how they came up to the fence and silently watched from a distance.

The paramedics worked on the body next to the still running lawnmower, they administered CPR and used a defibrillator, then carried the body to the ambulance at the gate. It drove away and the people watching slowly and quietly retreated from the fence into their gardens, while their dead neighbour's son, who had watched the paramedics until the end without moving, went over to the still running lawnmower and from there, from the very spot where his father had collapsed and died, from the exact place of his father's death, continued mowing the lawn in the direction his father had presumably been heading.

Lies have always become me, I always look best when I'm most devastated, he said. And it was true. Mr Gärtner sat in bed before me and looked marvellously recovered. Whenever anyone told me to my face how good I looked, I was always, in fact, on the brink of suicide. We prove ourselves true to our lies, so take a good look at my face.

I had invited him to move in with me and, not surprisingly, he'd refused. There's not enough air for both of us in your place, you're misjudging the situation, he said, because fundamentally you're just like all the others.

It takes strength to carry your own weaknesses. Neither of us has enough, that's our bond and it protects us from each other.

My early years belonged to someone else, Mr Gärtner said, my childhood was one long delusion. It was good to be mistaken for someone else, at least for a while, and then no longer. My parents were never really mine and I was never their child. The wrong people brought me into the world in the wrong place and it was the same with those I'd found for myself, they were all the wrong ones, and I was the wrong one, too, I would never have chosen to be myself.

I began to doubt myself early on, he said, and with reason, only later did I despair. A sense of calm settled in with time, after years, a sense of contentment, actually, to which I slowly began to reconcile myself, complacency, obtuseness, this calm was the worst of all possibilities. Take my advice, be on guard against yourself, resist your own self as long as you have the strength.

And now, as you can see, I've opened the curtains and I'm looking out again. I've even opened the windows, I've decided to ventilate. This odour, you understand, having only my own air to breathe, nothing else, I couldn't take it any longer. As soon as I opened my mouth there was the stink of a bad conscience.

You chopped down the chestnut tree. I watched you from up here. I spent years of my life under that tree.

He looked over at his desk, covered with stacks of paper. Notes on failure, he said. When I'm disgusted by everything round me, I retreat into my notes. They've certainly piled up over the years. And yet, just one glance in the mirror makes the lot superfluous.

What is it I lack? A person, Mr Gärtner, they tell me, what you need is another person. And they're right, I've always felt that I, myself, were missing.

Nevertheless, I've got the constant urge to telephone—I should call someone, I always think here in this bed, I wake up and want to talk to someone. But then, whom could I call? So I don't call anyone. I had my phone disconnected.

This inner disquiet, this outer stasis, I'm facing the end and I mull over the beginning, over how it all began and with whom.

If you ever sell the house in Landskron, I'll rise from my grave. If you ever do that to Georg, I'll come after you, Anna had said to me on our last visit to the graveyard.

I'd never considered selling, not at the beginning nor in the months since. I'd settled into this place and Landskron had sucked me in, just as Anna had predicted.

This place has its living and its dead and I'd joined the ranks and become one of them and now belonged as I never had anywhere else.

The dead weren't gone and the living could not be driven off, so I'd have to live with them if I couldn't be alone. I'd begun to live with them, establishing myself here, digging in, setting down roots, like one of Georg's trees and no one could fell me but myself.

Night had fallen and I stepped into the boat and got a shock since I hadn't expected anyone to be there. The night was dark, there was no moon, and the lights onshore were turned off.

It was my visitor. She invited me into the boat; apparently she'd been waiting for me. Row alongside the reeds, she said, I like the sound they make.

We headed out to the monastery and back again. The water was rough and both of us were drenched by the waves. Again and again, startled ducks shot out of the reeds and flew out over the lake. In the darkness, our silence brought us closer.

The entire time, she tapped her ring on the side of the boat in rhythm to my rowing.

You know the feeling you get when you touch things that caused someone's death or that someone used to kill himself, she finally asked.

I didn't, but then I thought of the boat and the fact that Georg had died in it. Still, I didn't mention it and she suddenly withdrew. Back at the dock, she went up to the house without saying goodbye and locked herself in the room.

And then one day she left her door open again. On the table lay a handwritten note.

Inge,

I've always known what should have been done.

In all the years since then, I've had to live with my failure to do it.

But I won't any more.

Paul

Landskron is my parents' territory, family ground, anyway. It was always a place to avoid but one from which, in the long run, I could never escape. On the very same day I found that letter, I took it to my parents' house, even though I knew from the beginning it would be a mistake.

In their house nothing had changed in the years I'd been away. My parents had aged and their habits had aged with them. They greeted me by listing everyone still living and those who had died, just as they'd always done, and the list went on and on since we hadn't seen each other for such a long time.

In my family, there was always someone who'd just committed suicide or had just attempted it. My relatives are always giving birth or killing themselves off, they've always reacted to a problem by having a child, every difficulty, every hopeless situation brought a child into this world and there were always enough problems and hopelessness to go round.

My relatives die young or not at all. My grandfather was on the brink of death for years. For years, he'd get up from the table after dinner, for my entire childhood, in fact, it was always the same, I watched him carefully, he'd stand up and say, I don't feel well at all, then he'd say, this time it's serious, my time has come, I won't survive the evening, this night is my last. Then he'd say goodbye to my mother, my father and to me, he'd close the door behind him and wait for death, each night, and for years he didn't die.

In the morning, he'd come out of his room.

Maybe today is the day, he'd say, it's not so bad for me to practise, that way I'm prepared. I have a feeling it could be tonight, you know.

Rehearsing death, every day, in vain, all for naught, I got that from him.

Early on, I was fond of my grandmother. She took live chickens out to the chopping block and brought them back dead and from then on was no longer my beloved grandmother. That didn't exactly build a sense of trust. My grandmother I always respected but my grandfather I loved.

When, years later, her tongue swelled up one night at the table and she became mute, then and for ever, I understood that the house would never be the same.

And for a while it was true, we were surrounded with absence, her presence, actually. And then no longer. Everyone but Grandfather got used to it, I believe.

Then, when Grandfather died, I thought I'd never be able to go back in the house again without constantly feeling his absence. And for a while that was true, too. But then things changed, I eventually noticed that we managed without him, that there was no longer any trace of the panic, the fear I'd felt as a child when I thought that one day this house would be here without him, as it then was.

The dead linger for a long time but eventually they do leave, that's one explanation and that's evidently how it was here, in my parents' house, though not in my house in Landskron.

We sat across from each other, our silence leading from one misunderstanding to the next; the letter lay on the table between us.

We'd always been good at keeping secrets and now silence, again, was their answer to my question about Paul.

News from the realm of the undead, Mother said and set the sheet of paper back on the table. I knew immediately, when you moved into that house down in Landskron, that sooner or later you'd bring up something like this, she said and walked out of the house.

There are more and more reasons to keep silent, Father always said. You won't get anything from me, he warned me, I won't say a word on this subject, or only this much, the happiest men in the tavern are often the saddest men when they're at home, those who are the life of the party are unbearable at home. And Paul was, without a doubt, the sociable sort.

Georg held his tongue until the day he died. With us, silence begins at birth and we learn it as the family's language the way others learn to talk. Learning to talk for us has always meant learning to keep quiet, to keep secrets, in fact.

It's a small step from listening to someone to sounding him out. We knew how to insinuate or to hold back enough information to create a rumour, to spread slander, we were well practised in that. A sideways glance, a wink, a shrug was enough to have someone excluded, to make him disappear, even erase all memory of him.

A life frittered away in cafes is the sign of a thoroughly unhappy man, Father said and got up to leave.

I always forget that the dog is gone, he said, my hands are always feeling round under the table for the warmth of the dog that died a long time ago.

We walked past the house and through the village. All our walks eventually led to the graveyard and this one was no different. As always, he stopped at the railing on the wall and looked down at the graves for a long time. As a child, I'd always slipped away at this spot, I would keep going, running on ahead. The stopping and standing still, the endless gazing down at the graves was unbearable. This time, too, I wouldn't stand still and tried to steer him away from this spot, to lure him on. I quickened my pace and kept up a constant stream of talk. With one story after another I tried to distract him from the thought that he, too, would soon be lying there, even though I, myself, could think of nothing else the entire time.

I noticed that the graveyard had recently been redesigned and expanded. There were no graves in the new addition.

He didn't let me distract him. He went down the steps and crossed the still empty expanse to the exit on the far side of the graveyard, where I was waiting for him.

On our way through the village, whenever we passed an old man sitting alone on a bench, he'd say, I'll soon be sitting alone like that. When we got to the graveyard and were standing next to our plot, he said, not long now and I too will be lying there, in my grave.

I tried to dodge these thoughts as I would blows but I couldn't escape them; over the years I'd become too deeply imbued with them and now they were my own train of thought. A life with a future is something my father never had, from the very beginning our future was simply his fear of what was to come, his limping, his preoccupation with the fact that he, too, would soon be lying in his grave. Our future was always his approaching infirmity, which he had predicted all along. Eventually we passed a remote barn. A man stood in front of it looking at us keenly. I was struck by how confidently he stood in his field.

At that moment, my father pulled me aside. The business with Paul, he said, leave it be. You can't change anything. We've never been good at atoning for things, and we all have enough to atone for, who doesn't, but still, it's a relief not to have killed anyone, it's a relief not to be lying under the ground yet, just as it's simply a relief when you make it through an entire day without being guilty of anything, or towards anyone, not even yourself.

My mother was always saying, I don't want to live any longer. At every opportunity she'd say it and withdraw. Closing the door behind her, she'd leave the house and stay away, yet she returned after a while, every time. I don't want to live any longer, whatever she intended, whatever it actually meant, she wore the phrase out in the end, no one heard it any more or paid it any attention.

One day she took my hand and led me to a strange house. As we stood in front of it, she smiled at me, put her finger to her lips, unlocked the door and pushed me inside. Inside, everything looked familiar because I could recognize her in each object and I realized she was showing me her place, her refuge when she left us. Her refrain, *I don't want to live any longer*, suddenly had a new meaning for me. From then on it meant I don't want to live *with you* any longer.

And yet, after all, she'd let me in on her secret, I thought, so I must be part of her refuge and from then on her refuge would be my refuge, too.

I followed her into her secret and even began to make myself at home in that house. She didn't prevent me and I was too distracted and busy to notice that she'd left at some point. At first, I was annoyed when I noticed the door was locked. I realized she had locked me in and immediately made my escape. I climbed out through a window and ran straight home, where Father, unsuspecting, sat in his room. Yet this time, I didn't find his lack of concern reassuring. Why did she lock me in? I wondered and searched for her throughout the house. She doesn't want to live any longer. I went from one room to the next, to the attic, the cellar, out in the barn, and then went through them all once again, and back to her refuge, where would she do it? I wondered and ran into the forest, looking for her up in the branches. I wandered through the trees for hours but she was nowhere to be found, not hanging from any of the trees, which I hugged in relief but loathed at the same time, embraced and despised; each tree was my personal enemy, as was the forest as a whole, because it offered her an opportunity, a temptation, if nothing else.

Darkness had fallen and I understood that my efforts were pointless. I gave up and hurried back home, imagining how someone might come to our house that night and send me out of the room in order to tell my father something I was not meant to hear. When I got home, I opened the door and heard the clinking of silverware. They'd already sat down to eat, I joined them at the table and the food tasted better than it ever had.

My relatives are nothing more than a disease threatening to infect me. When I was young, I spent my time evading the adults, then I tried to avoid everyone in my generation, now I stay away from their children, and with good reason, since every encounter with them is and has always been a backsliding, a slip into accessibility from which there was and is no escape, not ever.

This sense of belonging with people you'd never sought out always horrified me, this feeling of not having chosen certain people, yet being forced to be one of them, without any hope of getting away, this sense of being tightly bound to each other through bloodless and withered family bonds, bonds through which blood only flows when you've cut yourself free. We wear these bonds like a noose round our necks and they draw tighter with each meeting or even at the very thought of a meeting.

The doctors claim I'll make it, just imagine, he said, it doesn't bear thinking about, if they're right. It just doesn't end. They aren't to be trusted, you know.

Mr Gärtner sat facing me on the dock, agitated as I'd never seen him before. He kept tugging at his waistcoat, pulling it this way and that, then straightening it out and boring his finger in one of the buttonholes, searching for something no longer there.

One day, the children take their parents into the forest, he said. It's big and dark. It has rooms and at night you hear screams coming from them. This forest is Hermagor, the old-age home, and Laas. This time I was in Laas. They tell me I tried to kill myself. They claim they have to protect me from myself. But that's not true, I'm alive, worse luck. Why bother killing myself, I ask you. They think I've given up. The truth is, I've become inured to myself.

We get used to everything in the end, even to ourselves, we make peace with everything and in the end with ourselves, too, even if it never works out. We're born and we scream and we're told to keep still. We open our mouths and scream and realize everyone wants us to be quiet and calm, so we close our mouths. We're silenced, stifled, made mute. In fact, we should never have stopped screaming, not from the beginning, not our entire lives, up to the end, one single, continuous scream. But we do stop and spend our lives dreaming ourselves back to life and have no idea what it is we're hoping for. A long sleep will refresh you and make you alert, we were always told, yet we sleep and don't wake up refreshed. We wake up one day in Laas. It's all just a dying away, falling asleep, waking, done.

He gazed round the property and out over the lake. His eyes lingered on the trees I'd chopped down, only to sweep back over the house, again and again.

What all haven't you destroyed here, he said, laughing at me openly. You've created one giant swathe of destruction, which for me is salvation, a liberation in any case.

You've done away with this Eden, finally.

This area, Landskron, it eats away at me like fear, he said. Georg cared for it and cultivated it, one giant construction, all of it, the greenery, the trees, the lake, Georg's longing for this paradise was nothing more than a longing for death, just a process of dying. I, on the other hand, resisted it to the end and nowhere else am I as resolutely alive as I am here.

That mountain over there, he said and gestured with his head towards the opposite shore, what does anyone know about that mountain? The dead have good memory. They wake us and drag us back to life. They can see everything from that mountain. From there, they remind us how easily we forget. And it is all idyllic, this mountain and the lake with the boats sailing by.

The Security Service had its training camp on that mountain. Their surveillance, the terror, began there. From their outpost up there, they monitored the lake and the surrounding area. And this house.

Georg and I always had that mountain facing us. That mountain grew from the pit we dug back then, he always said. The mountain stands there as a reminder, right in front of our door. It blocks our view and our vision, rightly so. Through all these years, Georg stared at that mountain, day and night.

I'm not complaining. I'm not defending myself, I'm guilty.

We're guilty and we want to be distracted from our guilt. We spend our lives searching for conformity but are horrified when we find it. We want to belong and if we really do manage to belong, we despair. All conformity leads to despair and every difference is an irritation.

And the boredom, the desolation, we inspire in ourselves, what wouldn't we willingly put up with just to escape it. Encounters, offences, actually, every encounter brings devastation.

And yet, we experience flashes of devotion, now and again, and even these days, still, this desire for dependence. We can't manage without others and we can't bear ourselves, we keep ourselves amused, although badly, we've got used to it and it's doing us in.

Today the lake is so deep, you see how deep the lake is today, he said and tossed one of the buttons from his waistcoat into the water. The fishermen who've anchored their boats out in the middle of the lake, look how they stare into the water. They row out there and set their anchors, each one has his own spot from the time they're just children, then they spend their lives staring down into that abyss without ever noticing it, not even once, because all they think about is the fish.

This lake is a trap, an ambush. They throw out their lines, their nets, they submerge entire trees down in the water. Under their boats, the sea is like a forest, a refuge for the fish and in this refuge, hooks lie in wait.

Under water they use the trees to lure the fish and on land the dead lure the living, there's a refuge for them here too, take a good look, so you don't get caught in it yourself. They're on the hunt for prey here, every one of them, they've set hooks out in every refuge. You know they don't want you here, he said, because your property was their hunting ground and free like the lake.

They're all on the prowl here. From childhood on they're trained, directed, focused only on hunting and fishing, on trapping, it's all entrapment, in fact. The pleasure they take in an ambush, their lust for prey, their instinct for killing, and you, yourself, you sit looking on from your dock and life rows past.

He looked up at the bay window again. The shutters had been closed for a long time because the woman had not come back since I'd found the letter.

What's left to say? What's left to say and to whom? he asked. What should we keep quiet and from whom? It might be possible with you, perhaps, you've got enough patience. You sit there without saying a word as if you, too, were lying in wait, and I respect that. So perhaps there's a chance for a fresh beginning, or one last attempt, at any rate.

Mr Gärtner looked over at one of the hedges. A boy stood hidden behind the fence. I'd seen him before. For weeks now, he'd been following me, not letting me out of his sight. He'd turn up at the most unlikely places and then disappear a moment later through one of the many holes in the hedge which I had taken for animal trails.

I threw a rock in his direction and he disappeared.

The boy's mine, he said. The truth is, he doesn't belong to anyone, he's abandoned, completely wild, you can see it yourself, but he has got good instincts and a pronounced preference for distance, distrustful, like everyone here, but he's not really bad and, above all, he's the only one here you can rely on.

The boy was back at his spot. Just ignore him, Mr Gärtner said, don't pay him the slightest attention, that's the only way to win his trust, though that kind of person will never trust you completely. But he's getting ready for you. He has chosen you, that is clear.

He needs a case he can study and that's what I am for him. He's yours when my time comes. In that way I'm his preparation for you. The thought of being found by that child one day I can't bear thinking about, but still, that's the way it will be.

Mr Gärtner sat lost in thought, without making the slightest movement. Do you like graveyards? he suddenly asked. He stood up and got ready to go out. You are fond of graveyards, isn't that right? he asked and took me by the hand. Let's go to Ossiach, to the graveyard there, he said.

A hearse blocked the monastery entrance. The vehicle's door sprang open and a group of pall-bearers climbed out cheerfully and began changing their clothes right there. They hung their suits in the automobile like gutted animal skins.

Grief always stands ready to be borne and is delivered to each and everyone, Mr Gärtner said as he led me past the pall-bearers and into the courtyard. We walked along the wall towards the graveyard. He stopped under an enormous sundial and looked directly at the sun. This courtyard, he said, how many purposes this place has served, as well as being renowned and notorious and feared, for centuries.

The sick were healed here. The mentally ill, the insane, they were set straight here, they were brought here from all over and set against this wall. They were tied to chairs and crystals were bound to their foreheads. The sun's strength was trusted to do its work. They were left in the sun until the demons escaped from the bodies of the afflicted through the holes burnt into their heads. Each of them arrived with a demon and was sent away with a hole in his forehead.

An empty cart was wheeled out of the chapel. A woman stood before it with a bouquet of wild roses and stared woodenly down at the cart. We greeted her but she ignored us.

The benefit of graveyards, he said, is that here, more than anywhere else, it's obvious that, one way or another, we'll all die one day. He walked slowly along the rows, pausing by each grave as if he knew them all. I stayed behind and followed him at an appropriate distance.

Missives of homelessness, he said, each name is a wrong address. You won't reach one another or, even worse, you do.

He finally stopped in front of one particular grave and didn't move for some time, then he waved me over. A sign was stuck in the dirt—*The plot owner is requested to report to the graveyard administration immediately.*

Mrs Gärtner perished trying to find beauty in this world. I'm the cause of her death. That's what people say. There's nothing they won't say.

She didn't want to live without having her own place, a plot in this graveyard. You'll have to bury me, she always said. And since then, whenever I come here, she's got me eating from her hand, from her fear. You look for someone so you can escape life's tedium, so you won't have to live alone, so you won't have to die alone or just out of convention, and then you end up destroying each other.

And all along you're plagued by this hunger, this insatiable appetite for whatever it might be, but at the same time with disgust for everything, a constant choking, in fact, that's the part of myself they should protect me from. Cawing madly, a murder of crows landed on the tower in the corner of the graveyard. Just listen to their screaming, he said, I can't get enough. But at some point silence falls and all is done.

Woken by the buzzing of a dying housefly, I got out of bed and went down to the lake. I had dreamt I was my father but I calmed down on the dock.

A small mound of mussel shells had drawn me to the dock. For a long time they'd lain there unnoticed but the pile gradually grew larger and in the past few days it had got so big, I could hardly miss it.

I assumed it was a gift, an attempt to make contact in any case because the shells were carefully arranged, like a sculpture. I'd avoided rearranging or even removing them altogether because of my suspicions concerning the *artist*.

He had been hiding under the dock and now surfaced among the reeds from which he watched my every movement.

I didn't want him to feel he'd been found out, so I wondered out loud where the shells might have come from and in what mussel beds new ones would grow since there were none to be seen at the bottom of the lake.

I left for a while and when I came back, a rock coated with tiny mussels lay on the dock. It came from the debris Georg had had dumped along the shoreline to reinforce it. I stepped into the water and took a few rocks at random from the piles, turned them over and saw they were all covered with minute mussels.

A gurgling sound came from the reeds and the boy disappeared under the water as if something had frightened him. I looked up towards the house and saw my parents standing in front of it waving at me to join them.

My father had apparently not missed the scene. I see you're not completely isolated, he said, that's good. You spend too much time by yourself and were always a loner. You got that from me and it's not a trait you can get rid of. I'm glad to see you're fighting it.

Paul's letter had had an effect and brought them here. They'd come to make sure everything was all right. People their age never leave the house without getting dressed up. You have to leave the house as if you might never come back, Father always said, you never know what might happen.

Georg's trees, the forest, he said. So this is how you thank him. It's no wonder folks here take you for what you really are.

I opened the door and led them into the house and into the havoc I'd created inside, which suited me perfectly.

Warily and on their guard, as if something might fall from the ceiling at any moment, they felt their way from one room to the next, becoming smaller and smaller until they finally shrank to their proper size.

The astonishment clearly stamped on their faces finally brought home to me the extent of the work I'd done on the house to this point. I'd eliminated all traces of my predecessors, I now saw, at least on the ground floor, but had spared the upper floor in deference to Inge. As for this house's dead and their relics, I'd taken them all down from the walls, pulled them down, dragged them out and buried them in the yard, sunk them in the lake or burnt them, as required. Then I had stripped and replastered the walls. I thought I'd painted over and erased everything that had been there but all I'd really done was whitewash it.

While Father anxiously searched for something he could connect with his memories, Mother went upstairs. How tactless, she said, ungrateful, as if you despised them all.

It occurred to me that we weren't alone in the house and I called up to her, letting her know, but it didn't seem to bother her or she just pretended not to hear.

Inge had come as I'd hoped she would because the house only felt inhabited when she was here. She belonged here more than anyone else, I was sure of it, even if I had no idea why this was so. One morning, after I'd repainted the boat and was about to repaint her name on it, she suddenly appeared, holding something out to me. This is Paul's pencil, it goes with the letter, she said and led me back to her room. I'm unhappy here but here no one notices. The feeling that others don't want me here makes me feel the same about myself and yet, nevertheless, by sitting here in this room, talking to myself, I finally feel that I'm present again, the letters I've buried deep inside are in easy reach once again, she said.

Father had given up looking for anything familiar and sat across from me on the only chair left in the room.

You're making a nest here for that woman, he said, and you wouldn't be the first to come to no good because of her. The letter, who could have given it to you, if not she? What does she say, what are people saying about us, and above all, what is it, supposedly, that was done to *her*?

The way you stand there, he said, it reminds me of Georg. Every conversation with him was a dissection, everything was dredged up and exposed, but the only subject Georg ever took a knife to and carved up was himself.

A thing or two, yes, people did know a thing or two but not enough to make them into accessories or accomplices. There was not enough substance, as you can imagine, no real food for thought, the only thing ever served up was silence, shame and disgust.

Guiltlessly happy, that'd be ideal, he said, or blamelessly guilty, if it's not possible to be without sin. He took my arm and led me into one of the rooms on the ground floor and up to the bed in which I'd been sleeping. This is where it all began going downhill for Paul, he said, here in this bed. Paul came back after the war and found his wife in bed with someone else, one of the occupying soldiers, then she left with him for England.

After that Paul always preferred being in the cafe to this house and from then on all he did was play chess. It was the beginning of his end. He really could have made something of himself but had no discipline.

There was a sound of knocking upstairs, growing louder with each rap. Mother had found Inge. But Inge wouldn't open the door—why should she—and Mother appeared at the top of the stairs. She doesn't recognize me, Mother said, or rather, she's decided she doesn't know me. Mother went back to Inge's door and tried again. She kept on knocking until I couldn't stand it any more and went up to get her. When we returned downstairs, Father was gone. Paul's letter lay crumpled on the chair.

My bed was a hill of moss. I lay in it and couldn't get out. A fence enclosed the area. A woman sat outside the fence, cradling a child in her arms. My view is obstructed and foggy but I can see her hug and kiss the child. The child squeals and wriggles with delight, squirming with pleasure under her touch. He twists and turns, leans away and then back towards her, putting his forehead to her lips and her neck, her ear and her cheek, her throat, and then twists away and she turns him to face her again, over and over, slowly, she turns the child and lifts him to her lips, then holds him out and brings him back to her lips, again and again. The child can't seem to get enough and leans towards her eagerly, her mouth opens and closes and I can see threads coming out of her mouth, each kiss attaching a thread, her lips roaming over his body, weaving a net round him that thickens and shimmers and soon encloses him completely in a cocoon that hardens into a crust, losing its shine. It is soon covered with velvety fur and turns the same shade of green as the moss I am lying in. The cocoon is woven round the child's entire body except for his mouth. There's still life inside him, you can see the cocoon pulsing for a while, then it stops. There's no movement at all, the child's belly lies flat and stays flat and his cheeks collapse in. The woman kisses the opening over his mouth. Nothing more than a gasp, a gurgling, comes out, now the child is still and does not move again. She smiles, cradles it, her movements slow down, then stop, she remains motionless for a time, then moves again, she comes back to life. She stirs and smiles in my direction, noticing me for the first time. She stands up and approaches the fence that surrounds me, this fence has a gate, a door, she enters, comes up to me and kneels down beside me. I watch as she leans over me, lays a hand on my forehead, over my eyes and frees me from the threads that had bound me. Her mouth is closed, then she opens it and licks the moss from my eyes, the threads disappear into her mouth. My head is now free, my throat, too, I can feel the air, the breeze, a light draught. I lie before her, under her, now she's digging me out, I think, but she stops at my neck and doesn't free my body. She stretches her hand out towards me, pats me along the length of my body and, at the level of my lap, begins digging a hole. She holds the child in one hand and digs with the other, then lays the child into the hole and buries it, humming softly and contentedly as she works. She bends over me again and rests her forehead against my cheek, then on my mouth. Her gaze falls on me like a shadow. Her lips are sticky and moist, she smiles, she closes her mouth and kisses me, raising and lowering her head, threads come out of her mouth and form a veil over my eyes. I can't see, I can't breathe, nothing more, done.

A fear of cellars, she said, a fear of other people, actually, that's something Georg always had in spades. Go look in your cellar for that fear. He was always one for cellars, that was his place and that's where you'll find him. Georg spent his entire life putting things aside, burying them, hiding them from others and from himself. Dig up your cellar, look in your attic, up in the rafters, or have you already? No, you haven't yet, have you? Otherwise you'd never have been able to throw out so easily and carelessly all the things that made this house what it was.

Inge had dropped her reserve after my mother's visit and came looking for me every day in one of the rooms where I was trying to get on with my work.

She stood for a while in front of one of the pictures I hadn't yet had a chance to remove. Like all the others, it was tilted. She straightened it.

Those pictures, there, take them out of their frames and you might find what I'm looking for or at least a hint about where I could find it. As for the walls they're hanging on, these walls are bursting with life, but you'll figure that out, she said. Pull up the planks, rip out the floor and dig under the floorboards, throughout the entire house, everywhere. I'm happy to help if you need me.

You just covered the old walls with fresh plaster, she said. You repainted the walls and refinished the floors but you didn't dare look beneath or behind them. It's all new but it's all still the same. The truth is you've just disguised Georg's hideout, as if he'd charged you with wiping out everything that might recall his time here.

You've made it too clean, I miss the dirt, she said and knelt down on the floor in front of me. She stuck a knife in one of the gaps between the floorboards, scraping it along the planks. She held out the blade, covered with the dirt she'd dug up.

Dust, she said, what do you know of this dust, whose shoes brought it in and what it means for me and for this house? Georg had a good memory and a bad conscience. You'll find both in these cracks, behind the wall and in the ground. They hang from the rafters like Paul's noose. Cut them down, dig them up and bury them properly, so that they'll finally be at peace, even if there is no true peace to be had.

The hatch door to the cellar closed over me and wouldn't open again. No matter how hard I pushed against it. It wouldn't move an inch. I felt round for a light switch. I found one and a bulb at the other end of the room flickered on, then immediately went out. I had seen enough to venture down into the cellar, at least I thought I had, so I made my way down the stairs and over to the shelves that filled the room, hoping to find a light bulb or some tool I could use to get out. But I soon gave up. My eyes still weren't used to the dark. I went back to the top of the stairs. I sat and laughed in the darkness because, I thought, if Inge hadn't put so much pressure on me, I wouldn't have fallen into this trap so quickly. The fear of cellars, fear of heights—these were familiar to me, too. Maybe that's why Georg named me his heir.

Up to this point, I'd been *cleaning everything up*, Inge wasn't wrong. I'd been *clearing it all out* in an attempt to free myself from everything that wasn't part of my story. But what I certainly wasn't doing was searching, because the last thing I wanted was to *find* anything. My own story was enough for me. Even then, I wanted to get out of my own story and to avoid getting sucked into a new one, which in this place would only be the same old story anyway. Still, ever since Inge had drawn my attention to it, I couldn't get rid of the thought that in my carelessness, I might have overlooked or thrown away something important. And if, in fact, I had become Georg's dogsbody, as Inge had implied, then I wanted to know how it had happened, what it had to do with this house and what it would mean for me from now on. So I did begin searching even though I had no idea what I was looking for.

I had repainted the walls, now I stripped them again. I knocked holes into the walls, exposing the beams only to plaster them back up, because there wasn't a trace of *life* to be found in them.

Then I'd started on the floors. I scraped a knife along the cracks between the boards, as Inge had done, and dug out the dirt collected there. I found nothing but now everything round me, things I'd barely glanced at before, looked suspicious. I examined it all closely, suspecting even the most trivial things of being hiding places, though for what, I couldn't say. I uncovered the debris piles I'd made in the yard and dug up the holes I'd carelessly filled with all sorts of things from the house. But all my efforts were in vain. I didn't find the slightest trace of Georg, only his trees, his garden, the walls of the house, his books and a few pictures. Everything that might have been essential to him had been disposed of *before* my time.

I'd stored his books in the shed my neighbour had tried to claim as his own. They were stacked along the wall on which the hare carcasses had hung. I leafed through each and in each I found only a smell of decay.

The pictures, Inge had said, take them out of their frames.

There were old prints of Villach, Landskron and the Landskron castle ruins, along with local landscapes and views of the lake and the monastery depicted variously in watercolour, oil and film. Two men looked at me from one of the photographs. It showed a boat sailing on the lake, heeling sharply, one of the rails almost completely submerged, with billowing sails. The men in the boat sat braced against the wind. A young Mr Gärtner looked at me complicitly over Georg's shoulder as he tightened one of the sheets.

When I took the picture down from the wall, it slipped from my hand and shattered and when I picked it up, a second photograph appeared behind it. It showed the quarry I knew from my excursion with Mr Gärtner. It looked exactly as I remembered it, the shrubs round the opening that had been blasted into the rock face, in front of which I'd paced while he lay in the grass, the swifts, the pine trees, not a thing had changed, as if the men in the picture hadn't grown old in the years since it was taken. Mr Gärtner's hand was raised in greeting. Next to him stood a woman leaning against the cavern entrance. It was Inge. Behind Inge stood a man about the same age whom I didn't recognize. His arm was draped round her shoulder and she seemed to be clinging to it tightly.

These pictures reminded me of the photographs Georg had taken of us each time we visited. My search for them led me to the cellar.

I went back down the cellar stairs to look about on the shelves. Empty bottles, bits of this and that. And, finally, a spade. On my way back to the stairs with the spade, the floor suddenly gave way and collapsed and I found myself up to my waist in water.

There'd been a dripping sound the entire time I was in the cellar but I hadn't paid it any attention. The drops fell gently and regularly from a pipe, no doubt the source of the pool I was standing in.

I waded to the stairs but before I'd given the hatch door even one blow, it was opened from outside. With a smile, Inge helped me climb out.

Told to go outside and pick cherries, I stretched out lazily beneath the tree and ate them. The shade was cool and refreshing, all was right with the world.

I helped myself from the basket I'd taken down from the tree. I put one handful after another into my mouth and spit the pits out in wide arcs onto the grass.

When a flock of young starlings circled the tree and went after the cherries, the peace and quiet was gone. A shower of ripe fruit pattered down on me and drove me out from under the tree. In my rush I stumbled over something on the ground not far from the tree and covered with twigs. At first I took it for a bird's nest with a few eggs but when I cleared away the top layer of sticks, I saw it wasn't filled with eggs but with a small mound of eyes.

I still had a cherry in my hand. I realized that it was a human eye and that the cherries I'd pressed against the roof of my mouth with my tongue weren't cherries either.

I looked up at the tree. Eyes hung from the branches singly or in pairs, even in clusters, and stared impassively at the grass. The birds pecked at them greedily.

I remembered that I'd been sent out to the tree to pick whatever I could find and so I hung the basket on one of the thicker branches and filled it with this *fruit*, the juice seeped through the weave of the basket, formed puddles on the ground and began to thicken. My work was finally done and the tree picked bare. Still, the birds wouldn't leave. They stayed perched in the tree, sharpening their beaks on its branches.

I sank my knife into the wall up to the hilt and the buzzing from behind the shelves, which had drawn me to this spot, swelled at first and then grew quiet.

Wasps crept from the crack into which I'd stuck the knife and ran busily up and down the handle before disappearing again behind the wall.

I wedged in a crowbar and wrenched hard. It was clear from the notches in the wood that I wasn't the first to go after this spot and I remembered that Georg had once disappeared into one of these walls right before my eyes. I'd been startled awake one night and had crept out of my room. I found Georg in the hallway working away at the wall with some kind of tool.

Alarmed, he shooed me back into my room. Hornets, he whispered, this house is one giant nest, and he warned me not to come near him. They're peaceable creatures but you have to take care not to excite them. Three stings can kill a horse, so be very careful and don't come out looking for me any more. With that he disappeared and for days was nowhere to be found.

I was sure I was standing at the very spot I'd searched for so often in dreams as a child and again in the weeks since returning to this house.

Three stings, one horse—that had made an impression on me and even though I was only dealing with wasps, not hornets, Georg's warning still made me hesitant to go after them. In the meantime, they'd multiplied and spread throughout the house in such numbers that it was unliveable. Their buzzing came from every gap and crack in the house. They were everywhere, in the laundry, in bed and in the closets. Finally it became impossible even to work in the house. At the slightest disturbance they flew out from behind the walls and swarmed after me.

I had to do something about them. I pried the trim from the wall and saw that the trim had in fact been used to fasten the board underneath to some planking and that this planking was a door. I pulled the door out of the wall and the wasps swarmed out, chasing me through the house, from one room to the next. No matter where I tried to escape them, others were already there, ready to attack me. I ran down to the lake and swam to the other shore. When I finally ventured back hours later, they hadn't stopped looking for me.

That night I tossed a petrol-soaked rag into the hiding place and boarded up the entrance and by morning the gas and the stink had done its work.

More than a few of the wasps had slipped out through the cracks and hung like seething felt on the wall round the edges of the planking.

I shone a light into the hideout. It was a small chamber, a niche, actually, extending the entire length of Ludwig's room behind which it was hidden. A folding camp bed, a table and a chair. Georg's cell, I thought and went in.

The dust from old wasps' nests lay ankle-deep on the floor. The walls appeared to be covered by a kind of plaster with countless clusters of little pustules blanketing the entire surface of the walls up to the ceiling. The wasps fed the larva in them and fluttered their wings sluggishly.

The bed was folded up and completely covered with these little cells.

The table had several drawers. I pulled one out and found Georg's photographs.

Please follow me, my name is Strametz, I'll kill you. I followed the man into the house after he had stopped me on its doorstep. The doors to the rooms along the hallway were all open. In these rooms, elderly people lay on beds and pallets, more than a few of them strapped in.

I had found a note on my dock, weighted down with a mussel, *Mr Gärtner, Serenity Lake Nursing Home, Room 110*. One floor up, the doors were all closed but one. Mr Gärtner stood alone in the room, looking out of the window at the lake.

A suitcase lay open on the bed, as if he had just arrived or was packing to leave.

Now they're taking me away from myself, he said. Whatever happens, will happen without me. *We've got to get you to a doctor. We've got to test your blood, your heart.* That's how it began. This time it's my head. *Serenity Acres, Serenity Lake.* Just a matter of changing beds, of being moved from one grave to another, actually. But really, it's all preparation for Laas.

They put this man in the room with me. *At your side*, they told me, *so that he can attend to you.*

Mr Strametz had sat down in a part of the room that was apparently his and rustled his newspaper busily without taking his eyes off us for a second.

Every day this man asks the administration to let him stay one more night, Mr Gärtner said. For him this place is a hotel. He's been here for ten years now. Every day they allow him one more night.

In return, he watches me. His duty is to *protect* me and he takes his duty very seriously. Mr Strametz has all but quarantined me. He won't let anyone near me and because of that, my forays into reality have become rare.

I promised him I'd intercede with the administration if he made an exception for *you* and allowed you to visit.

Mr Gärtner picked up his suitcase and walked out of the room.

The final journey, the two of us, together, he laughed. You've come to take me away. To Landskron, to the castle. I'd like to see it one last time. From there I'll continue alone.

We were stopped at the entrance and were only allowed out once I signed a form stating that I would bring Mr Gärtner back to the home that same day.

He didn't say a word during the drive. He held on tightly to the suitcase on his lap and stared straight ahead without moving, not taking the slightest notice of the landscape he had claimed he longed to see one last time.

A few days before, I'd gone to some of the places that were recognizable in Georg's photographs to compare them to the past that was preserved in his pictures. The photographs lay in the glove compartment, right in front of Mr Gärtner. From the way he ignored the pictures, it was clear that he recognized them.

We had covered most of the distance and were just passing a pond when he suddenly opened the car door and insisted on getting out and walking the rest of the way.

The pond was overgrown with bulrushes and reeds. A path ran along one shore and led to a bank on the other side.

Mr Gärtner nodded towards the bank and began walking down the path. I stayed behind briefly, then decided to circle the pond as well but in the opposite direction. The path was so marshy and overgrown that I was soon reproaching myself for letting him go on alone.

He was swallowed up by the bushes again and again and then seemed to sink into the reeds but he didn't give up and slowly made his way to the bank. When he finally reached it and sat down to rest, he waved me over.

Why did Georg choose *you*? I wonder. By choosing you, he must have wanted us to meet one day, he said. What bound you and Georg, what is it you have in common and, above all, how are you two different? Why *you*? I wonder.

We spent our childhood on this pond, Georg and Ludwig and I. And Paul.

From the bank there was a clear view of the castle, I noticed.

Whenever you spend time observing something, what you end up watching is the process of disintegration, he said. Just look at those ruins. In Landskron, they let everything fall apart and out of every ruin, sooner or later, up sprouts an inn.

We made our way to the castle ruins.

Nothing looked familiar to him in the castle courtyard. It was completely rebuilt and remodelled and the routes he wanted to take through the castle were barred with gates or chains.

We finally retreated to an oriel window with a view of the entire valley. Mr Gärtner gazed for a long time at Villach, at Landskron and at the western bay of the lake, looking at each in turn, again and again. The quarry, in particular, affected him deeply.

You found Georg's photographs, he finally said. You're well informed, that's good. The sailing boat in the picture in your car, the English confiscated it after the war, the house, too. They took everything Georg owned. Georg was *tainted*, you see.

I went back to the car to get the photographs. I'd found stacks and stacks of them in Georg's hideout.

The entire extended family looked out of the pictures, laughing. The young faces of all the other *candidates* to the house, posed in front of the wall, in the wood and under Georg's trees or while planting the trees that were now gone, just as more than a few of these candidates had disappeared as well. They'd ended up in front of trains or in the water and those, like me, who were still living had turned into their own fathers and mothers.

Pictures of the dead, laughing. Back then even despair seemed entertaining, at least it looked that way in the pictures. And I, another dead man among many, I belonged with them, in the past and since then, even now. I was no different from them, not in the slightest.

Many of the pictures were of Georg and Anna with their friends in the house or in the nearby surroundings, on the dock, in the boat and in the reeds, alone or in groups, *together*, always laughing, carefully posed, in changing seasons, the same people, pictures of a happy time, it seemed.

Most of the pictures were taken while travelling— Genoa, Capri, Palermo, in vineyards and under palm trees, in front of churches and ancient columns, in ports and on boats, Messina, Agrigento, Florence.

Postcards Georg had sent to his mother on those trips were glued into the album among the photographs. Signed by Anna and him.

Anna was in the centre of the pictures, Inge mostly off to the side, facing slightly away, yet *she* often appeared to me to be the true subject of those photographs. The more I looked at them, the more I was convinced of this.

One of the postcards was from Inge, posted to the same address, sending greetings to Georg's mother, from Ludwig and her.

I returned with the photographs. Mr Gärtner was sitting at the same place, looking out towards Annenheim at the peak of the Gerlitze.

The noise from the valley had grown louder. Chain-saws, traffic.

The sunny shore of the lake was always the louder one and it still is to this day, he said. The shady side was always the poor side. When someone from the sunny side married someone from the shady side, it was always considered a misfortune, a step down, in any case.

Inge was from the sunny side. The shady side didn't do her any good either.

Mr Gärtner had rested his hand on the album for a long time. He finally opened it, only to snap it shut again immediately.

Most of the photographs were of Inge and the man I recognized from the one taken at the quarry.

Portraits of a great devotion, a dependency, actually, he said and pushed the album slowly across the table. I never had anything to offer except insecurity and empti-ness, weaknesses and emptiness. Georg and Ludwig were no different. And Paul, Paul was one giant void, a void he drowned in one day.

Each person you open yourself up to, every meeting with someone new is a birth, a new beginning, but the truth is, it's just the beginning of something you'll destroy. It's nothing more than that, never was, never will be. You lure someone into your own abyss, wanting a future together, you know, and then you see them drowning in this void. So you leave because it is unbearable to watch.

On the other hand, there was always pleasure in it, too, a craving, actually. It meant you were alive and that was worth a transgression every time.

You're filled with longing for another person but you spend your life trying to avoid meeting him or her, so you won't be disappointed again. Your entire life, you wish you were dead and yet you resist death at the very end, an endless watching and waiting for death to finally come, only to flee at the final moment.

There's a time when something happens. There's a time when it's done. I've always liked going to places where something significant happened to me long after it's all over and done with, when it's ancient history, even for me, he said. Anywhere, that is, except here, not with Georg and Ludwig and Inge. *Preserved feelings.* It's all long gone, yet, everything is still the way it was.

I'd pushed an album across the table. It recorded the construction of the house. He picked it up and leafed through it for a while.

How faded my life looks to me, he said. Georg's brothers and I built the house together. It was a fixation of ours, we had a lot of fixed ideas back then but this one we actually followed through. It was the first house in the whole area. Before we built it there was nothing, only forests and scrub and the lake, magnificent wilderness. The neighbouring houses came later, little by little. Now it's overdeveloped.

The lot had to be cleared first, you see, you know the process.

He placed the album open in front of me and leafed through it slowly, forward and back. At first glance, you could only see a dense forest. But if you looked more closely, you could make out a few men here and there with axes and saws.

Each picture was labelled with the year it was taken.

A few pictures on, a clearing had eaten into the wilderness, then a mound appeared which turned into a pit a year after that.

That mound ended up in the lake.

Rails led from the pit down to the water. Carts filled with dirt and rocks were pulled along them with ropes.

Every year the land extended a bit further into the lake, he said.

There were pictures of men with picks and shovels levelling the hill and extending the shoreline and of men sawing and planing the beams and boards with which, one picture and one year later, the dock and the boathouse were built.

Pictures taken from the dock showed the foundation and the frame construction, then, finally, the finished house with those who had built it standing in front and Georg, Mr Gärtner and Inge waving from the bay window.

It was in this house that things began between Inge and Ludwig and it was in this house, when they came for Ludwig, that things ended for all of us. After that everything went downhill with the house and its occupants. The wilderness crept back and reclaimed it all and when Georg returned from captivity, he didn't have the strength or the will to fight it. On the contrary, he contributed to the property's decline. The state of the house mirrored the deterioration of those who lived in it, trying to get on with their lives but only falling apart.

Supports, handles and handrails sprouted everywhere, from the house down to the lake, along the stairs inside the house, everywhere, old-age home equipment; it was horrible. Every year, there were new frailties and new railings for them. Georg hated these things but he had them installed anyway because he depended on them more and more.

You've freed the house from them, Mr Gärtner said. You're restoring it to its original condition. But it's still derelict, no matter how much work you've put into it.

He pointed out one particular construction worker again and again in the various pictures, as if he were trying to tell me something. But he just sank back exhausted. Mr Gärtner seemed to collapse before my eyes. He's pulling back, I thought to myself, but a moment later, he'd got a hold on himself.

Paul wasn't much good at choosing friends, he said. It was Paul who brought this person in. Of course, there was no way Paul could have had any idea that one day the man would be a snitch for the Gestapo. As a carpenter he knew every corner of the house. He was involved in the planning, so naturally he knew about the secret room where Ludwig hid for a while. This man is the one who gave the tip that led them to Ludwig.

That wasn't Paul's fault. Paul trusted him. We all did. And who could have expected something like that? No one. But Paul couldn't live with it.

Then Mr Gärtner put his finger on the face of the man in the picture before him and traced the contour of the man's body.

Paul was not one for elaborate funerals. He made sure it wouldn't come to that.

With that, Mr Gärtner closed the photo album and looked me directly in the eye.

What difference does it make if you leave? Or if you stay? Ludwig didn't come back after the war, that is, he did come back but only to leave for good. He disappeared since. They all left. Ludwig and Inge. And Paul, in his own way. Only Georg and I stayed.

Over the years, Georg seemed to have come to terms with what happened to Ludwig, at least he worked hard to give that impression, but he never made peace with himself.

Mr Gärtner flinched suddenly, as if in pain.

My body is giving out, he said. I'm thinking in years but only have days left. This contradiction helps me face things I otherwise couldn't bear thinking about and it's making me talkative once again.

I don't want to make you my conscience but still, you'll stay, at least until my time comes. Look into my eyes, the life of a dead man, take a good look. Cut into me as into an open wound and you'll have all of Land-skron before you.

Blood flowed from the tap but I only realized it when I saw the stains on the hand towel. I looked in the mirror. My face and my hands, my throat, everything was smeared with red.

I couldn't believe what I was seeing and tried to make it go away by ignoring it. I turned on the tap and held my face under the stream of water but the smears wouldn't wash off.

The old pipes, the rust, the darkness are tricking me, I thought and went into another room and tried the basin there. Blood flowed from all the taps and the scabs in the basin began to loosen with the fresh liquid.

I rubbed myself raw with a towel and the pain awoke me. I made my way to the cellar because I suspected the pool of water down there was at the bottom of my anxieties.

The dripping hadn't stopped, and why would it, the pipes leaked and needed to be replaced.

But first I had to clean out the cellar. I couldn't manage alone so I brought in some help. I let the workers take whatever they thought was still useful. The rest lay in the yard a few hours later. A pickup drove up to the piles and when almost everything had been loaded into it, an overstuffed bag slipped from the hands of the man standing in the truck bed and fell at my feet.

Without thinking, I kicked it aside and it burst open and papers flowed out. The workers weren't even out of the house before I had the sheets spread out in front of me on my desk. At first I was only interested in the photographs I'd pulled out from between the pieces of paper. Rosental, Maria Elend Church, St Jakob, Rosenbach, railway stations, barns and many pictures of the forests surrounding the local villages. Feistritz, Unterbergen, Loibltal and the Karawank mountain chain, Loibl Pass and the tunnel I often drove through to get to Slovenia.

I kept rearranging the pictures until I finally ordered them into milestones along the route south from Landskron to Loibl.

Most of the papers were mouldering documents from the war and the years right after. Pages torn from books, handwritten notes and newspaper articles about the Loibl tunnel and about a *work camp* run by the *Waffen-SS*, which I'd never heard of before reading about it in these articles.

Prisoners in this camp built the tunnel, I read. They'd been *selected* from Mauthausen for this work and brought to Loibl, political prisoners, mostly Frenchmen at first. The goal was a connection to Yugoslavia and *extermination through work*. Officials pressed hard for both. *Replenishments* were sent from Mauthausen. They were often necessary because the labour camp soon proved too small. A second camp was built and *deliveries* were received from Mauthausen. The *materials* were Poles, Yugloslavs and Russians, Austrians and Germans, Belgians, Norwegians, Hungarians, Algerians, Spaniards and Greeks.

Deliveries were also made in the opposite direction. Those *unfit for work* were sent back to Mauthausen for *extermination*.

The camp doctor determined on site who would be sent to Mauthausen or to the *infirmary* by *ambulance*.

A beautiful death, the camp doctor said years later, *an injection of petrol to the heart. It was all over quickly. Transport to the infirmary, anaesthesia and injection.*

They burnt the corpses in bonfires.

The camp was built on a mountain slope. Every day the prisoners left the camp, climbed up the side of the mountain to the tunnel site. Only the ambulance was more feared than the construction site because in the ambulance death was all but certain.

The dead were left lying in the open, for all to see, until the next shift. At night the bonfire was lit.

From the tunnel site they were sent into the tunnel, in *shifts*, and then back out, past the dead bodies and down to the camp with a large piece of rock strapped to their backs.

The kapos were encouraged to beat the prisoners and they fulfilled their duty with rubber hoses full of sand and iron filings.

At night *ballets* were performed *to balance out the work. Encouragement* was offered with whips and hoses. Screams could be heard on the farm not far from the camp where the SS gathered to drink and dance with the local girls.

On Saturdays, the *Lagerälteste*, senior camp inmates, went hunting with the *Blockführern*, senior block inmates. To the *corrida*.

The prisoners had to dig ditches and then fill them. The guards began beating them and launched the corrida by driving their victims through the camp to one of the barracks. They forced their victims into the building, then bolted the windows and doors. They stripped the prisoners and dragged them onto a table that had been pushed into the middle of the room. They stretched each prisoner out on the table, held him by the arms and legs and by the head as the kapos came up to do their *duty* until the body on the table stopped moving. The body was then dragged off the table and thrown into a corner and the procedure began again, from the top, one body, the next, one Saturday, the next, then roll call and back to work.

Sports, exercise, ballet.

The tunnel was opened to traffic in late 1944. Three years later there were photographs of the henchmen on the dock.

Death by hanging. Life sentence. Twenty years. Twelve years. Acquittal.

A life sentence meant a few years, then it was over. The country had to be *rebuilt* and they didn't want anyone left idle, not even the camp doctor, who was soon back in his practice.

I didn't know what to do with this find but I could not escape it either. Someone who had lived in my house had studied this camp and its history for decades and had compiled this collection of documents. Whoever it was, it wasn't Georg alone because many of the documents originated after his death.

I died when they entered the room, she said. It was noon. Outside, a light rain was falling and I had just closed up the entrance to Ludwig's hiding place when they suddenly appeared in the room. I knew that I'd led them to Ludwig.

It was summer. The end for all of us had just begun but we didn't realize it yet. We hadn't been in touch with each other for quite a while because they were already after Ludwig at the time. Landskron was being monitored. I was under surveillance and Georg had forbidden me to go anywhere near the house. But still, I came here looking for Ludwig and delivered him right into their hands. I was the one who brought Ludwig into this whole story and they took him away instead of me. I hadn't been in the house long when they came asking about him. He's not here, I said and that seemed to satisfy them. They searched the entire house and disappeared but a moment later they were back, right in front of me, this time near the hiding place. They came in and pulled him out before my eyes.

I began laughing, she said, and only stopped long after Ludwig had been taken away. I went out of the house, closed the door and left this place, the whole region, and didn't come back.

I sensed Inge's reserve even though she had come to trust me. For me, at any rate, she was the first and only person before whom I felt something like shame, although I didn't have the slightest idea why.

I had put a few of the pictures and newspaper clippings in her room too because I assumed she would help me. And in fact, soon after that, she came to find me. We had driven over to the sunny side of the lake and were looking back at our side.

Our origins are our downfall, she said after gazing for a long time at the house that had been *our* house for a while now. That's something Georg always said and you don't seem to disagree or you wouldn't have destroyed everything that was entrusted to you here. And yet, even so, you want to know what happened, at least you seem to.

She looked at me intently. Your parents, she asked, your relatives, what do they say about me? Do I even exist for them? What stories do they tell about me?

Ludwig ended up in Mauthausen. From there, he was sent to Loibl.

He survived. He made it. But he never came back. I don't know why.

Once, years later, I saw him coming out of a bar in Klagenfurt. He crossed the street to a phone booth and I watched him as he spoke with someone. After he left, I went into the phone booth and as I watched him walk down the street and finally disappear round a corner, I held the receiver to my ear so I could feel his warmth again.

Let's drive, she said, we both loved the places on the way to Loibl. And we set off in that direction.

In St Jakob she directed me towards a hill with a church that was visible from a distance and that for years now I'd wanted to visit every time I drove past.

We had just got out of the car and were looking up at the church when a group of men in black uniform emerged from one of the nearby houses and headed in our direction.

A few of the men had dogs. They held their dogs on short leashes. One of the dogs was free. It began baying and ran away from the group towards us. It barked at us and ran in circles round the two of us, occasionally pushing at us with its muzzle.

The other dogs strained at their leashes, pulling the men towards us. It wasn't long before they'd formed a circle round us. Their dogs, now all off their leashes, circled us, barking and leaping at us and snapping at my coat, which I'd draped over Inge's shoulders. The men acted as if we weren't there. They continued their conversation and gave their dogs free rein. There seemed to be no end to this nightmare, so I opened the car door and pushed Inge inside. Only then did I notice how terrified she was of the dogs. Looking at her you couldn't tell, but she was completely rigid.

The pack drew away abruptly and the men headed off, laughing. They all climbed into a car and finally were gone. They didn't look back at us once.

Inge no longer wanted to see the church, so we continued on our way through Rosental. Maria Elend Church, then Suetschach. Past Feistritz we stopped the car and Inge led me along a field to a copse. There was a bench next to it and we sat down. She looked at the fields in front of us, at the forest and over towards the border.

They hunted men here, she said. Rosental was one of the *movement's* regions. The valley resisted. A borderland, you understand. And it was *our* spot. I lived here with Ludwig for years. Here we weren't surrounded by all the people who were otherwise always round us.

After a fashion, this place became *my* spot, too, after my time in Landskron. Hundsdorf, St Johann, Rabenberg, I'd been retreating to these places more and more often in recent years after Landskron had become unbearable and each time I came, I found this landscape strangely soothing.

There was a sign indicating the way to Loibl but I didn't want to go there unless Inge asked me to. She had seen the sign, too, and yet she told me to head towards Hollenburg Castle which had just become visible on the other side of the valley. That's where we're going now, she said. I turned the car and we crossed the Drau River towards the castle.

They caught the camp doctor on the old Drau Bridge, she said, he'd gone undercover and wanted to cross the Drau here to get to Klagenfurt. A former prisoner recognized him.

The castle was open for viewing. It had a gallery and Inge made her way through the rooms with the same sureness she'd shown at our first meeting at my house. The museum guards didn't keep us from any part of the castle and so, after several hallways and flights of stairs, we finally reached *her* room. Another place from my past, she said. A sitting room. She went up to the window and gazed at the view for a long time, then waved me over. The entire valley spread out below us along with the Drau, the Karawanks and the mountain roads leading through them and the road to Slovenia, of which we had just turned off to get to the castle.

Ludwig's route to the camp began at the Klagenfurt railway station, years earlier, she said. Early one morning we were heading back to Villach after spending the night with some friends. It was cold and we'd been waiting a long time. The first train had been cancelled and the second was delayed. We didn't dare leave the station because we absolutely had to return to Villach. For hours we were the only ones on the platform except one man who had got off one of the trains that had come and gone in the meantime. Like us, he seemed to be waiting for the connecting train to Villach.

When we learnt that the second train would also be cancelled, we gave up and left the platform. The man came up to us and ordered us to show our papers. Destination, departure city, addresses, where we'd spent the night, with whom, he wanted to know everything and he wrote it all down. Then he searched Ludwig. When he'd finished and was turning to me, a train pulled into the station, jerked to a stop and began to pull away again immediately. The man left us abruptly, jumped onto the train and didn't take his eyes off us until we were out of sight. The train seemed endless and took a long time to pass through the station. I saw the door of one car swing open and two men walk up towards the front of the train. Everything was moving very quickly but I did see that the second man was in handcuffs and was being dragged forward by the first man. When the first man yanked open the door to the front car, the prisoner threw a bundle of small pamphlets onto the platform. The door closed behind him and they were gone.

Around midday we were finally sitting on a train. On the way Ludwig whispered to me the contents of the pamphlet, which he'd memorized in the toilet. It was a call to resistance and he was more than a little surprised when I prompted him with the passages he couldn't remember.

Up to that point, I'd never spoken to him about my ties to the resistance group I had joined. I didn't want to get him involved in anything that seemed so uncertain. I was also afraid of asking too much of him. Still, I'd been waiting for a long time for an opportunity to finally tell him.

I told him everything but all he could hear was that I'd kept it *secret* from him until then. It all began with those pamphlets, she said. I gave him the contact that he himself had been looking for and from that point on he was part of our group and very active.

The appeals were printed in Klagenfurt. Some of the material came to us from Slovenia and Italy and was distributed by railway workers who travelled across the country.

He was taken away and we kept on without him, until the end, but I still haven't come to terms with the fact that I was spared. As if all they really wanted to do was separate us—I still can't shake off that suspicion.

Inge and I left the castle and continued our journey. We soon passed the sign to Loibl but without turning off this time. Piles of scree lined the road, and piles of dirt, a house flanked by chestnut trees that reminded me of the railway station near where I grew up. The road's incline grew steeper and we passed isolated houses, a small village, then we were on the mountainside in Unterbergen.

The prisoners left the camp, she said. In the very last days of the war, they marched down this street from Loibl into the valley. They spent the night in the railway station and went on to Feistritz the next day. On the way there, they were officially liberated by the partisans.

The next village, Unterloibl. The road became steep and winding and the forest came right up to the shoulder. At the junction to Bodental there was a chapel. Inge got out of the car and went into the chapel. She stayed for a long time.

The road descended the mountain in hairpin turns to a ravine and then rose again. There were no houses for a long stretch and then an inn, *German Peter*, with a vacancy sign. The engineers were housed here while the camp was being planned, she said.

Inge didn't want to stop here. The road kept rising, occasionally a shack stood by the side of the road, abandoned, run-down, surrounded by the forest from which shots rang out time and again.

The colours of the flowers, autumn in the larches, the beeches, snow on the cliffs farther off, this truly is a glorious landscape, and yet when I think of having to live here, I immediately have the urge to end it all.

At the border, dogs were brought to our car. They sniffed it over and were taken to the next car. The guards waved us through and we drove into the tunnel.

Inge got out at the southern mouth of the tunnel, on the Slovenian side, and I followed her to a viewpoint, a terrace with a telescope set in its centre. Wood and karst, steep snow-covered cliffs, eroded, fissured, under avalanches of scree, a barren, inhospitable region.

At first we couldn't see any trace of the camp from the slope we were standing on. There was a church and next to it a house with smoke rising from the chimney and a small castle behind them.

The camp was built on property owned by Jews, Inge said. The land belonged to a baron who was murdered in Mauthausen. The site managers were housed in the castle. From there you could see everything.

I looked down the mountainside.

You won't see what you're looking for, not from here, she said, there's a forest in between. She was right. I could make out a fence and the remains of a wall. There was nothing else to see. The scene looked like an archaeological excavation.

We headed towards the site and after just a few curves in the road we came to a kind of lay-by. Tables, dustbins, benches, and on the other side of the road, a memorial I didn't remember seeing on earlier trips through the area.

The enclosure was bordered by a low wooden fence. Cows grazed in a field nearby and the sound of the bells on their necks could be heard from quite a distance. The slope was terraced and some of the level spaces were covered with cement, others with grass, the foundations of houses and the remains of walls. The impression I'd had of the site from a distance was not wrong.

Clusters of larches had been planted in the field along the fence.

Inge had sat down to rest on a bench.

A panel depicted the site and described the original layout of the camp, of which only the stone foundations remained. Stairs, cement steps that led into the barracks grew out of the grass and ended in the open air.

The *Appellplatz*, the roll-call area, was now a lawn studded with an enormous number of little mounds of earth, molehills, the entire field had been dug up by moles and reddened with the freshly exposed dirt.

I went from one panel to the next, each posted in front of a particular relic. *Barracks, kennel, latrine, SS troop barracks, arms depot, infirmary.*

Here and there were those clusters of larches. I went up to one and found the base of a watchtower sticking up slightly higher than the grass amidst the trees.

Officers' barracks, bath, barber, field for football and boxing matches.

Near the *infirmary*, I heard the sound of a running stream. I followed the noise. I left the fenced-in area through a gate and walked along a descending forest path.

Reddish water flowed over the stones. When I dipped my hands in the water I noticed a pit not far from the stream that I hadn't seen at first and I went up to it. It was covered with an iron grille. A grate. A trough drained the pit into the stream. I stepped into the trough and pushed away the leaves that had collected in the water. They circled the stones for a while, then disappeared.

A child's screams drew me away. As I returned up the forest path and along the fence towards the *infirmary*, I saw a young family coming towards me across the roll-call area. A man was pushing a pram in which a child screamed incessantly. The woman led the way and read out the text on each of the panels while he tried to quiet the child. A girl followed them at a slight distance.

The wind had picked up and stung my ears. I looked over at Inge. She was sitting motionless on the bench. The girl drew the outline of a game in chalk on the floor of the *bath* and hopped about in front of a chimney.

After a while I reached the south end of the camp and from there I looked up at the church and the baron's house and then again at Inge, but she had already left.

The young ones go to the cinemas, the old ones to the graveyard, Mr Gärtner said. We've already been to the graveyard and we don't want to go to the cinemas, so let's go on an excursion, provided Mr Strametz will allow it.

He had moved to a room one floor below and was ready to go when I arrived, as if he had been expecting me.

Here I'm finally at the mercy of the doctors, *senile dementia*, they tell me, *recalcitrance*, that's reason enough for them to keep me here. *Preliminary signs of a natural death*, I've practised it long enough, he said, and now they're using it against me.

I had brought him a bag of mussels. On the dock, a second pile of mussels had grown next to the first pile. It was surely meant for Mr Gärtner. I brought him part of it and laid it on his bedside table but he took no notice.

An unpleasant area, he said, everything reminds me of Laas. But it will all play out for me in Heaven soon enough. However, to get there, I've got to run the gauntlet of doctors. Before, I had them eating out of the palm of my hand. Now they won't even look me in the eye. I hear them talking about me and as they do, they no longer take any notice of me. At some point, the people here give up and grow backwards into their childhood as they age. The nights here are a perpetual moaning and groaning. Fear stammers in the cots.

Every night I have the feeling that the next day will finally bring my misfortune and on the following day, I'm certain I was right. To sleep without dreams, without memories, to wake and then go through it all again from the beginning. Hope, yes, there is still hope, but there's no longer any justification for it. I'm shining a light inwards, into myself, but my inner darkness illuminated is pitch black.

They keep the doors open here and put flowers everywhere. The odour of death the flowers give off insinuates itself into everything, you can't avoid breathing it here, it's the odour of bodies lying in state, actually, of fear. Still, sooner or later it all becomes unendurable.

He glanced at Mr Strametz who sat listlessly on his bed, staring at the window.

Mr Strametz lives with me now, Mr Gärtner said, as long as I'm here, he'll spend the nights in *my* room, at least, that's what I promised him.

I left the room to get rid of the flowers I'd brought from his garden. In the hallway I pressed them into a nurse's hands and when I came back into the room, Mr Gärtner was sitting on his bed with the mussels on his lap. Just look at this, he said, a present. He was studying the shells so closely that for a while it seemed he wanted to examine each of them individually, but finally he put them carelessly aside.

Remembering is an act of forgetting and a fraud from the beginning, he said, still, many things are better explained with a lie and that's what does us in.

With that he stood up and I followed him out of the room. Leaving is the best arrival, he said, so let's go.

The boat we boarded in Ossiach was called the *Ossiach*. A wedding party had rented it but we were allowed on as well.

Mr Gärtner insisted we stand on the upper deck despite the cold and wind. The celebration was being held on the deck below. There were speeches, dancing and laughter and the music carried a long way over the water.

A heavy snow had fallen the night before. On the sunny side of the lake they were burning the vegetation on the train embankment, the entire shore was one smouldering band.

Mr Gärtner had wrapped himself in a blanket and sat at a table in the windiest corner. He seemed to enjoy the wind. A glass of wine in front of him, he was looking at the surrounding landscape and at the boat.

There were boats like this before, too, he said. After the war, the English used them for duck-hunting. There was constant shooting back then.

The boat had touched in at Bodensdorf, Heiligengestade, Sattendorf and finally pulled in to Annenheim, but no one had boarded or disembarked at any of the stops. The tourists were long gone and the area round the lake had calmed down.

Now and again, the wedding guests left the celebration and appeared on the deck but soon returned to the party since it was too cold to stay outside for long.

After a while, the boat set out again, heading towards the middle of the lake and then towards Ossiach. The music had stopped and all was quiet and for a while we were alone.

Mr Gärtner gestured with his head in the directions of Treffen and the quarry. Every place is the scene of a crime, he said. We were standing in front of the cliff wall in the quarry, Georg and I, on the day they came for Ludwig. One day an acquaintance of Ludwig's whose sister had been taken away spoke to him about the resistance. From then on Ludwig was convinced *he had to do something*.

Georg was on the other side, you see, and I was too. We couldn't see what was going on right in front of our eyes, not at that point. Georg tried to talk Ludwig and Inge out of it, he warned them again and again that people were on their trail, someone had told him in secret. Georg did everything he could to cover for them without them knowing about it. He got into a tight spot because of it. The warnings turned into threats and he passed these on to the two of them but they wouldn't give up, even after the situation had become hopeless. *Kin liability*, fear, you understand, and this mutual friend, this snitch, Georg trusted him. The authorities were supposed to come to the house, just as a warning, but they weren't supposed to *find* anything. It didn't work out that way.

On that day, we had gone to the quarry. We knew Inge would be followed if she actually dared go to the house. And she did.

Paul would never have allowed it. After he found out, he never got over it. Paul was very fond of your mother and his death hit her hard. She was close to doing herself some harm because of it, Mr Gärtner said. And I remembered searching the entire forest for her.

Someone came out on deck again, this time it was the bride. She walked past us to the railing, where she stood alone for a long time.

A man following her stopped at the top of the stairs and did not take his eyes off her. He went up to her and they fell into each other's arms. She threw her bouquet into the water and the man turned away and went back to the party.

The scene evidently did not escape Mr Gärtner. Things are still the way they were, he said, Georg and Anna celebrated their wedding on the *Landskron*. And yet, Georg only truly loved *one* woman in his life. And that woman was not Anna. The sorrow of the wedding guests who had heard, Mr Gärtner said, or who, like me knew the whole story; nevertheless we all celebrated with them on that day. I was the best man. Again, there I was, a witness, and again, I did nothing to prevent it.

The boat had drawn level with my house. There was light in one of the rooms.

Inge is looking out at the lake from her bay window again, he said, that's good, even if it won't make anything right. The two of them did what had to be done. And later, in the entire time since then, I never had the strength to appear before her as if awaiting judgement.

Darkness had fallen and the boat's lights were turned on. The party had moved to the deck and, laughing, the bridal couple danced past us.

The boat docked in Ossiach. Fireworks were set off and they lit up the monastery.

To stand in the reeds, he said as if to himself, to stand there as long as it takes to become part of the scenery, to grow into the scenery, like a post driven into the water, and to wait until the birds come and land on you, there is nothing else to wish for.

I didn't want to go to my parents' house and yet I went. My father had promised I'd learn something that would make it worth coming, so I set out to visit them.

All Souls' Day, All Saints' Day, actually, the relatives spend the entire year avoiding each other and then, one day a year, they all come together. On this day, they leave their houses and their valleys and gather in my parents' house to honour their dead.

By the time I arrived, the celebration had already begun. As I always had in the past, this time, too, I arrived a little late and, as always, no one took any notice of me for a while because in our family absence is always registered and remembered. The same groups had gathered once again, as they always did, and those who always stood off to the side were standing alone this time too. The laughter of reunion, embarrassed laughter, in fact; their mouths made the rounds with kisses and their voices spun delusions that blanketed the silence that has bound us together from the beginning.

Drinks in hand, they talked at each other. They have nothing to say to each other but they bray past each other, unimportant people, each self-important and each smirked at by the others. They understand one another when it comes to the preservation of their fears and they're lifeless, dead long before their time. Fertile parents, they reproduce and die off. They revere their own children and disdain the children of others. They despise suicide but study each case for their own exits. Their lives are determined by grace and disgrace, which they grant one another or pin on one another like a badge of guilt.

And I, myself, am the offspring of these people, not one whit better, I am one of them, I thought to myself and leant against the wall. From their glances, I could tell I'd been standing next to the wall for a long time.

Our dead came alive in stories that fit them to the truths we'd always wanted for them. My family talked about everything under the sun and they laughed at everything, too. But they never said a word about Georg or Ludwig and Anna and Paul. The past in Landskron was a topic they had never discussed and never would. The present had always been more than enough to feed their unhappiness. It rooted itself within them and spread to anyone who came into contact with them. Their unhappiness had no need of the past to thrive.

Bearing candles and wreaths, we proceeded to the graveyard. We stood at the graves and waited for the priest to work his way along the rows. In the stoup at my grandparents' graves, the holy water was frozen. Flies were trapped in the ice as in amber. Children lit the candles, everyone made the sign of the cross and we left. On the way home, I ended up walking next to my father. It seems Ludwig is in Laas, he said, I thought you should know.

I couldn't take too long to decide what to do because I knew I would talk myself out of wanting to visit him. So I set out for Laas right away.

I knew every inch of the road. Whenever we visited one of our own in Laas, we always made a pilgrimage afterwards—Birnbaum, St Lorenzen, Luggau—and if there was no one to visit in Laas, we made a detour round it because no matter where things begin for us, they always end in Laas, except for those who bail out on the way. But for the rest of us, Laas is where we meet even if only to part for good.

When I arrived at Laas, I saw that the house still stood on a rise in the wood but nothing else was the way I remembered it.

I drove along the wood and got out of the car. I walked the last stretch and inside I went from one floor to the next. I didn't want to ask for Ludwig, so I looked everywhere, but his name was not on any of the doors. I finally gave up and enquired after him. At last, I was standing in front of his door in an adjacent wing. The door was open. I entered his room, went up to the window and looked out through the lattice, over the fields at the village church. A light wind blew in through the cracks and shifted an enormous number of dried-up flies' and spiders' legs round the windowsill. The shadow of the trellis stretched across the floor, along the wall and onto a bed and the man asleep in it. He lay under a light blanket. Only his head was uncovered. And his hands. All the men in my family have such hands, I thought and examined his face. This woke him. He looked me in the eye and with a slight movement of his finger gestured at me to close the curtains. When I turned back to him, his eyes were closed and it was clear that I didn't belong there. I wrote my name and telephone number on a piece of paper I found next to his bed and left.

In the hallway, I was stopped by an angry nurse who only calmed down once she realized I could be considered a *relation*. Ludwig's car had been discovered on a dirt track nearby and he himself was found unresponsive inside it. He was no easy patient, the nurse told me, very tight-lipped, but it's not serious. He'll pull through.

Suicide. First, you should fall out with everyone, so that no one will be hurt, Mr Gärtner said and smiled through the netting they now protected him with. My last effort will be a refusal.

His wrists and elbows were bandaged and his arms and legs were tied to the bed. The mussels I'd brought him on my last visit were piled on his bedside table.

Heaven lies six feet underground. I'm on my way there, at last, and the doctors are helping me along, he said. They hold me back only when I finally have the strength and enough clarity to actually do it.

His fingers brushed the netting then gripped it tightly for a moment. A branch outside the window dropped its load of snow and sprang upwards against the glass.

I've come from Laas, I said. He didn't take the opening and I thought to myself, he's leaving me behind. He's moving on and leaving me alone with his story.

Mr Strametz' bed was empty, I finally noticed.

My life has been one protracted suicide, one endless thought of suicide, even if others round me died in my stead, Mr Gärtner said. Those letters, *Dear parents, I couldn't wait any longer*, letters never sent and never fulfilled, out of consideration, out of cowardice, actually. And so I waited, always. I waited for my parents' death so they wouldn't be destroyed by mine. I waited for my wife to die, for Georg's passing, all I did was mark time and wait, only to lose my nerve in the end. It's all horrifyingly familiar, everything has been thought and said a thousand times and nothing changes, not in the slightest, this desire to no longer have to listen to yourself, to be able to put cotton wool in your ears against your own thoughts. To wake up one day and no longer be dead, that would be the thing.

Mr Gärtner went limp and was no longer conscious of me. I ran out to the hallway to find a nurse but he was alert again and called me back into his room. He brought his head as close to the bars of the bed as the binding allowed him and I saw how much the effort to speak cost him.

The boy, he said, looking at the mussel shells, I know I can't ask it of you but, still, make sure the boy doesn't come to a bad end.

I nodded and left the room. I looked back at him from the doorway. He shook his head, smiling, and lifted a finger as if in farewell.

The ice will hold, I thought, and ventured a bit further out onto the lake. A light wind blew through the reeds, making the rustling sound I loved. From the dock I'd noticed a boat stuck in the ice some distance away. Two men were sitting in it. They seemed to be rowing but made no progress.

I was heading towards them, when a noise distracted me. It came from the undergrowth covering the slope to the house.

A body rolled down the embankment and landed in the reeds. It was naked and lay without moving. I didn't turn back but kept on towards the boat without taking my eyes off the body. Suddenly it sprang to life again and rolled out onto the frozen lake to a darker patch of ice, into which it sank and disappeared.

When I got to the boat, it was empty, abandoned in the ice, and there was no trace of the two men.

I could see now that the ice was red at the place where the body had sunk under the surface. By the time I got there, the hole had frozen shut and the water under the ice was red. Below, people drifted past, inert, or moved towards me and gestured at me to come down and join them.

I lay down on the ice to get a better look and saw a woman's face, her eyes open, she drifted up to the sheet of ice and, with a smile, waved me towards her. I put my forehead against the ice and shielded my eyes from the light. The woman's hands clawed at the ice. She stuck out her tongue and began licking it and I could feel the ice swallowing me; I sank, and the water sucked me in gently. I didn't resist because the water was warm and felt good, but when I was finally completely submerged, the woman had disappeared, as had the other bodies. A current pulled me away from that spot. I let it carry me and drifted away, but the water grew colder, frigid. I wanted to get out and tried to get back to the place where I'd fallen in but could no longer find it. When I was finally washed back to that spot and looked up at the surface, ice had closed over the hole the way bark grows over a wound on a tree.

There is one place I need to go, Ludwig said and pointed towards Kötschach. We drove there, down Gailtal towards Villach.

Just before Dellach, we were stopped by a herd of calves that had broken out of a nearby paddock and were running anxiously all over the road. Two men herded the animals towards several trucks, into which they disappeared before our eyes.

Grafendorf, Reisach, family sites, for me they're burial sites, there's at least one of us laid out in each place round here.

Ludwig wanted to see the hospital in Hermagor. Whom is he thinking of, I wondered. He sat motionless next to me, polite, proper, looking out at the landscape.

We drove past Pressegger Lake and came to a side road that led over Windische Höhe Pass to Villach. I wanted to know finally where we were heading so I turned onto the side road. We don't want to go to Villach, he said and so we turned round and got back on the road to Nötsch, making a detour round Villach and continuing into Rosental.

He didn't say a word the entire time. I sensed he was making the trip *alone*, into his own past, and I was not a part of it.

At St Jakob I drove up the hill on which Inge and I had the experience with the dogs a few weeks before. He got out of the car and we went up to the church. In the graveyard, he went from one gravestone to the next. After a time, he followed me back to the car. We passed Feistritz and I halted where Inge had asked me to stop because I felt he should know that I'd heard part of his story and from whom.

This time I stayed in the car. Near the bench to which Inge had brought me last time, Ludwig walked back and forth for a while, constantly looking from the forest to the border and back again, just as she had done. When he came back to the car, something had changed inside him. He was less guarded and he smiled at me. I see you're familiar with this place, he said, and that's good because now we don't have to speak.

He seemed to be scratching at his hand, as he'd done all through the drive, but now I realized he was just turning his ring round and round on his finger.

As we neared Loibl, Ludwig withdrew into himself again. With each curve in the road he retreated further inwards and finally sat apathetic and listless on the passenger seat, as if impervious to everything round him.

At the border we were waved to the side and asked to show our passports. A guard disappeared into his booth. Through the window I could see him making copies of our passports and entering the information into a computer. When he handed them back to us, I saw that Ludwig was a Swiss citizen.

I didn't know which side of the border he wanted to be on and my uncertainty caught his attention. He gestured at the tunnel with his head. We drove into the tunnel and down to the camp.

The fields were covered with snow. Ludwig's frailness vanished completely. He left me behind and struggled through the snow in the camp. He crossed the field and walked off towards the wood. He's going to the stream where I found the ditch, I thought to myself and looked up at the church and the house of the Jewish baron who had been murdered and sensed how deeply I was immersed in a story that was not *mine*, and I drove back through the tunnel to the Austrian side.

There wasn't the slightest trace of a camp there, only trees and bushes. Spruces, with shallow roots, I thought. Everything had been removed and the camp levelled. Only a few panels mentioned it in a few sentences.

I used the panels to orient myself and climbed a flight of stone steps that led to a clearing from which a farm could be seen on the opposite slope. It was no doubt the one Georg mentioned in his account. A ditch separated the site from the slope. A forest path led to it. I followed the path and came to an open space, at the centre of which a sign was posted: *Restricted forestry zone. No entry.* I entered the restricted zone. After just a few metres, I discovered a dark patch in the snow next to the path and when I cleared the snow with a branch, I found the remains of a wall, about knee high, covered with moss and frozen ferns.

An icy wind blew across the ditch, making me more and more uncomfortable. I drove back across the border to get Ludwig who was already waiting for me at the far mouth of the tunnel. On the way into the valley, he remained inaccessible. Every curve in the road caught his eye, every shack, too. Occasionally he shook his head slightly, at times he smiled. He appeared to have made his peace with something, at least it seemed so to me.

Past Unterbergen, we were back in the valley, facing Hollenburg Castle. I looked at Ludwig enquiringly, trying to gauge if he wanted me to drive up to the castle but he shook his head and laughed, kneading at his hand, which now had no ring.

Weeks later, I went to visit him in Laas. There was a new name on his door and a stranger looked out at me from behind it. Ludwig had already left.

A nurse called me back as I returned to my car. Mr Reger had asked her to give me something. A letter, she said, he asked me to keep it for you, in case you came back and asked after him. She went into the home to get it but couldn't find it. It's disappeared, she said. I followed her into the nurses' lounge, the *on-call room*, as she put it, but none of the other nurses knew anything about the letter. They searched their lockers but it was nowhere to be found, no matter how much I insisted they find it. Mr Reger handed it to me as he was leaving, she said. *For Mrs Winkler* was written on the envelope and he wanted me to give it to you and ask you to pass it on to her.

Annoyed, I left and drove to Kötschach and on into Lesachtal because I did not want to return to Landskron.

Why did he do it? I asked myself. Why did he leave the letter for me instead of sending it directly to Inge? I objected to the fact that whether or not Inge got Ludwig's note depended on me, especially since I'd never told her I'd been in touch with him.

I reached Luggau but still couldn't calm down, so I turned round and drove back in the direction I'd come, past Laas and through Gailtal, along the road I'd driven with Ludwig.

I've lost one more person in Laas, I thought, once again I've missed someone there. How often had I driven there, to that place, to visit one of our own, to haunt them one last time? We meet in Laas and we part ways in Laas, our solitudes are interchangeable. You just have to find yourself someone and in Laas that's not hard.

I stopped in Nötsch and drove over Kreuzberg Pass to Drautal and down to my parents' village.

Landskron had turned me into a *family relation* again. I could feel it but didn't want to accept it, so I continued past my parents' house to the railway station nearby and watched the house from there. My relatives left the house alone or in groups and strolled round the yard. I couldn't hear what they were saying but their laughter reached me across the distance. I finally saw my mother as well. With a finger to her lips, she stood in the doorway and waved them all back into the house.

A young couple was saying goodbye near the station entrance. The man disappeared through the door and the woman stayed behind. We'll see each other soon, she said, as if to herself, already walking away.

Ludwig no longer existed for me and I had another goodbye to say, this much I knew and I headed back to Landskron.

Greifenburg, Sachsenburg, Paternion, I took every available detour and yet always ended up back on the road to Villach.

I didn't want to meet Inge now, what could I possibly say to her, to this day I have no idea, and so I drove along the sunny side to the southern end of the lake and from Steindorf over to the shady side, past Ossiach and past Mr Gärtner's house. When I finally reached Landskron, I found a skinned hare hanging on my door with a note pinned to one of its legs, inviting me to dinner. I unhooked it and went off to retrace the route I'd taken with Mr Gärtner and with Inge. I looked first at the castle, then down into the valley, at the frozen lake and over to the quarry, at Annenheim and at the mountain Georg had stared at from his window for so many years and again at the castle and the lake and the quarry, the ponds, the mountain and every boat on the lake—all of these were Georg and Anna and Inge and Ludwig, Mr Gärtner and Paul, and all of it history, except me.

And yet, despite everything, this place, this region here round the lake, has become *my* place and *my* region. I belong here now since I've come to myself in Landskron in a different way than anywhere else.

You're only truly *at home* where you've got someone in the graveyard, Anna had said. I have my dead here and Inge will stay with me because, in truth, she made herself at home in Landskron long before I did. When I opened the door to this house, I opened a door into her past and I made a place for myself in this past and now I'm unable to leave it.

You're fond of graveyards, Mr Gärtner had said to me. I thought of his comment now, on my way to visit him. In Ossiach, I stopped at the monastery and waded through the snow into the graveyard. I stood for a long time at the grave of the monk Georg had told me about, the one who had repented a murder in the cloister. The crows whose cawing Mr Gärtner loved alighted on the field behind the graveyard wall and screamed continuously. Then, finally, all was still for a moment and I heard a noise like the flapping of flags. I followed it and discovered a mound of fresh dirt on Mrs Gärtner's grave. It was covered with mussel shells and the flowers decorating it were frozen. The bows on the wreaths fluttered gently in the wind.

At some point silence falls and all is done, I thought, as the cawing washed over me in waves.

This book has been selected to receive financial assistance from English PEN's Writers in Translation programme supported by Bloomberg and Arts Council England. English PEN exists to promote literature and its understanding, uphold writers' freedoms round the world, campaign against the persecution and imprisonment of writers for stating their views, and promote the friendly co-operation of writers and free exchange of ideas.

Each year, a dedicated committee of professionals selects books that are translated into English from a wide variety of foreign languages. We award grants to UK publishers to help translate, promote, market and champion these titles. Our aim is to celebrate books of outstanding literary quality, which have a clear link to the PEN charter and promote free speech and intercultural understanding.

In 2011, Writers in Translation's outstanding work and contribution to diversity in the UK literary scene was recognized by Arts Council England. English PEN was awarded a threefold increase in funding to develop its support for world writing in translation.

www.englishpen.org